LOVE AND LITERATURE

Love and Literature
Book 1

Aviva Orr

Dearest Reader;

Thank you for your support of a small press. At Dragonblade Publishing, we strive to bring you the highest quality Historical Romance from some of the best authors in the business. Without your support, there is no 'us', so we sincerely hope you adore these stories and find some new favorite authors along the way.

Happy Reading!

CEO, Dragonblade Publishing

This book is an homage to Charlotte Bronte's *The Professor*

PROLOGUE

Leave my loneliness unbroken!—
Quit the bust above my door!
Take thy beak from out my heart,
and take thy form from off my door!"

—Edgar Allen Poe, "The Raven"

Dartmoor, Devonshire 1850

*S*OMEONE OUGHT TO *tell them Mama is dying. But Papa doesn't have the courage, and I don't have the heart.*

Violet shielded her eyes from the emerging sun and squinted at the two children racing across the purple-hued hills. They zigzagged their way down the craggy slope, which came to rest a few feet from the backyard of their thatched cottage. Sebastian led the chase, churning the mud thick from that morning's rain. Frances followed on her brother's heels, but her gangly legs failed her, and she fell face forward. Violet groaned, thinking of the clean frock Frances had put on that morning.

The little girl leapt to her feet and shouted after her brother. Sebastian turned and waved something in Frances's direction, prompting her to sprint after him with renewed energy. He reached the bottom of the hill and raced home, barreling through the wooden gate that did little to distinguish their backyard from the tor-covered moorland beyond.

"Oh no, you don't." Violet eyed Sebastian's caked boots as he clambered towards the cottage, and she moved to block his entrance to the kitchen.

Sebastian charged forward like a cornered ram, forcing Violet to jump out of his way. Frances raced up behind him and flew past Violet.

"Do stop," Violet pleaded, following the chase through the kitchen and into the front hallway. "Don't," she warned in a low voice as they made for the stairs, but neither child paid heed to her.

Frances pursued her brother as if possessed by a demon. "Give it back, Sebastian! You'll crush it." She caught him by his shirttail and pulled so hard that she almost ripped the fabric. He stumbled and fell onto the middle landing of the staircase. Frances pounced onto his back, pinned him face down on the stone floor, and pried at his closed fist. "Give it to me! It is a special gift for Mama."

"Finders keepers," Sebastian taunted. "*I'm* going to give it to Mama."

Violet gritted her teeth, stormed up the stairs, swooped down, and pulled both children to their feet. They stared at her wide-eyed, their dark curls hanging loose and wild about their faces.

Although only two years younger than Violet, her ten-year-old siblings were so different from her that she sometimes wondered if they were changelings. Never would she leave her honey-colored hair a tangled mess or cause her clothes to become caked with mud from questing on the moors. She preferred to enjoy the bleak tranquility of the heath and the adventures found in books. But with Mama confined to her sickbed these past months, she'd had little time for such luxuries. No longer could she read for hours amongst the rustling golden peat. She'd become the woman of the house and had taken to securing her neatly woven bun under Mama's large bonnet. This added to her serious disposition and gave her a small measure of authority over her siblings.

"What is the matter with you two? Have you forgotten that Papa requires silence to do his work and that Mama is in dire need of rest?"

The twins glanced toward the top of the stairs where their mother lay in the sickroom.

"Sorry, Violet." Sebastian opened his hand and offered up the precious object—a small, blue speckled egg.

Violet shrank back from the ominous thing. "That's a raven's egg." Ravens were harbingers of death—everyone knew that.

Except for the twins.

"It's just an egg," Frances explained. "And it's not from a nest. I found it laying on the heath. And then, Sebastian—" Raucous coughing sounded from the sickroom above, drawing Frances's attention. "Mama," she wailed, snatching the egg from Sebastian's open palm, and sprinting up the stairs.

"No!" The word escaped Violet's lips in a frightened whisper. She dashed after her sister. But she was too late. Frances burst into the sickroom, threw her arms around their mama's skeletal frame, and pressed her lips against the dying woman's blood-spattered cheek. Violet gripped Sebastian's shoulders as they stood, frozen in the doorway of the room, and watched.

THE CONSUMPTION DID not linger for months in Frances's young body as it had in their mother's. Instead, it ravished her from the inside like a rapacious beast that happened upon a succulent kill. Three weeks later, Violet clutched Sebastian's hand as they stood at the edge of the cemetery and watched their father bury Frances and Mama side by side. She wished Papa were standing here with them, holding her and Sebastian close. But the sole comfort he offered was to say, "God works in mysterious ways," before leading the mourners into prayer and laying her mother and sister to rest.

She let her eyes roam the cluster of mourners. Neighbors, wearing various shades of shabby black, had emerged from every corner of the parish to pay their respects to the vicar's kin. They offered Violet no comfort, only pitying glances. Her aunt, who had traveled from London to grieve her sister, wept into a black lace handkerchief, and looked out of place in her elegant bombazine dress. Her husband stood stiffly beside her and threw disapproving glances at his wife's relatives and their congregation of unrefined mourners.

Violet squeezed Sebastian's hand in a show of support but received no response. She squeezed it a second time, but his hand remained limp in hers. She glanced down at him. He stood motionless at her side, staring ahead, his face devoid of emotion. It was as though his soul had fled his body and joined his sister in the grave, leaving an empty shell on earth.

CHAPTER ONE

A poor relation–is the most irrelevant thing in nature–a piece of impertinent correspondency–an odious approximation–a haunting conscience–a preposterous shadow, lengthening in the noontide of your prosperity–an unwelcome remembrancer–a perpetually recurring mortification–a drain on your purse–a more intolerable dun upon your pride–a drawback upon success–a rebuke to your rising–a stain in your blood...

—Charles Lamb, *Poor Relations*

Eleven years later
London, April 1861

THE AIR HAD a malodorous weight to it. Violet wrinkled her nose but resisted the urge to shield her nostrils with her hand. She'd been warned that the streets of London teemed with pickpockets and thieves, and she dared not release her grip on her carpetbag. A carnival of people jostled past her as they entered and exited Paddington Railway Station. They hurried about their business, seemingly unperturbed by the commotion surrounding them. But the clamor made Violet's skin prickle with discomfort, and she half wished she were back on the solitary summits of Dartmoor, where only the whistling winds trespassed on her privacy.

She edged forward and peered at the array of carriages and cabs that lined the street. How would she locate her aunt's carriage amongst such confusion? Doubt crept into her mind as she watched one horse-drawn vehicle after another arrive and then depart. Perhaps Aunt Prudence had forgotten all about her. Or worse, maybe she'd changed her mind about receiving her? It would not surprise Violet. The woman had paid no heed to her for the past eleven years, and Violet was skeptical about her sudden change of heart.

"Miss Greyson? Is there a Miss Greyson here?" Violet turned in the direction of her name, relieved to see that her caller was one of two coachmen atop an elegant, four-wheeled carriage. Both wore black top hats and navy-blue coats embossed with gold buttons. Her caller, the younger of the two, stood in his box seat and shouted her name into the crowd. His partner, a senior gentleman, sat holding the reins.

Violet hurried forward, but before she reached the carriage, a young woman emerged from the mass of people and stepped in front of her.

"I'm Miss Greyson," the woman said.

Violet hesitated in confusion. Then a moment's panic propelled her forward. "I am sorry, there must be some mistake. *I* am Miss Greyson."

The two coachmen peered down at them with creased brows. Then the younger man sighed and alighted the carriage. He beckoned Violet with his finger and bade her stand beside the other young woman. She drew closer and glanced at her competitor. Although young, the girl's skin wore an unhealthy pallor, and her eyes appeared sunken from what looked like a lack of sleep and malnourishment. Violet looked down at her travel-worn boots and felt the fatigue in her bones. No doubt, she didn't fare much better in her appearance.

The coachman opened his mouth to speak, but before he could address either young lady, a third woman thrust herself between Violet and her competitor, pushing them aside like

Moses parting the Red Sea. "Did I 'ear you call for a Miss Greyson? That carriage will be for me then."

The woman wore an indecently low-cut, bright orange dress and an equally indecent amount of rouge upon her cheeks. Violet thought she might be an actress. Were these people involving her in some type of live street performance that ensnared innocent pedestrians?

The coachman folded his arms and peered at the newcomer. "Is that right? And where is it we're supposed to be taking you in this splendid carriage?"

"Anywhere you fancy." The woman jiggled her breasts close to the coachman's face, and he grinned.

Violet watched the scene with fascination—not an actress but an unfortunate. She had heard about such women, but she had never encountered one.

"Oy!" The second coachman, who watched the events unfold from the driver's seat, dismissed the woman with a wave of his hand. "Off with you, strumpet!"

She responded with a rude hand gesture and then spun around. In doing so, she came face-to-face with Violet's first imposter.

"Lucy Evans! Fancy seeing you 'ere. Plannin' a trip in this fine carriage, are ya?"

The girl narrowed her eyes.

"This 'ere is Lucy Evans." The harlot turned back to face the coachman. "She's a genuine little miss. Can read and everythin'. Used to work as a governess in a grand 'ouse until the mistress caught her fornicatin' with the master." She chuckled. "Now she earns her keep at night, workin' the streets. Ain't that right, Lucy?" The harlot turned again, but the girl had disappeared into the crowd as though she had never been there at all. The woman cackled, winked at Violet, and said, "Good luck to ya." Then she pressed back into the throng.

Violet shuddered.

The coachman grinned as he watched her go. "Fine looking

woman that. Fine looking."

The older coachman, still seated in the driver's box, cleared his throat loudly.

"Right." The young coachman peered at Violet. "What proof have you to show us?"

"Proof?" Violet blinked in surprise.

"That you are indeed Miss Greyson?"

"What proof do you require?"

"Where did you come from, and what is the address of your destination?" He folded his arms and waited for an answer.

"I came from Dartmoor in Devonshire, and I am going to the home of Sir Richard and Lady Astyr. It is located in a place called May—" she hesitated—"Mayfair, I believe. Lady Astyr is my aunt," Violet added for good measure.

"Your aunt?" The coachman eyed her austere homemade black dress and frayed carpetbag.

She lifted her chin. "That is correct."

He raised his eyebrows in apparent disbelief. "Our instructions are to escort one Miss Violet Greyson to the Astyr residence, but I'll wager you are no more Lady Astyr's relation than them two harlots were." He jerked his thumb toward the crowd.

Her cheeks burned in response to the insult. "If you must know, my mother and Lady Astyr were sisters."

"Must be a poor relation," the coachman mumbled, although not softly enough to go unheard.

Violet paled. His words covered her in a veil of shame and pressed a wound deep within her. She stared at the navy-blue, gold-trimmed carriage that awaited her, keenly aware of her orphaned status. She claimed but one living blood relative in this world—her estranged aunt—upon whose charity she now traveled.

The coachman reached for her bag, and Violet stumbled backward, startled by the intrusion into her thoughts.

"I need to load this atop the carriage, miss."

Violet wrapped both her arms around her carpetbag and drew it to her chest. "If you don't mind, I prefer to keep it with me."

The thought of such an odious person handling her precious cargo made her insides tremble. The bag had belonged to her mother and ensconced within its threadbare walls lay everything that mattered to Violet—locks of Frances's and her mother's hair, Sebastian's worn copy of *The Iliad*, and her father's Bible.

The coachman shrugged. "Suit yourself." He opened the carriage door and made a sweeping gesture with his hand.

Awestruck by the carriage's luxurious, black-buttoned leather and blue-velvet interior, and conscious of the coachman's eyes on her, Violet sat down cautiously, taking care to keep her back straight and her head up. Only once the carriage door closed and the coachman returned to his seat did she dare to rest her head against the soft leather. She breathed deeply, thankful to be free of the odors that had assailed her out in the open. But she found it impossible to relax.

A forward-facing window gave Violet a clear view of the box seat, and she stared at the two coachmen's backs as the carriage rolled onto the street. The younger one's words still burned in her brain, inviting doubt. Why had her aunt sent for her after all these years? Neither she nor her uncle had paid any heed to Violet or her family after her mama's death. They had not even attended her papa's funeral. That had been a little over a year ago. What could have changed?

She turned her head and gazed out the window on her right. A grimy film clung to the air, shading the world in a hazy gray, and reminding Violet that she was a long way from home. The procession of horse-drawn vehicles she'd seen at the station continued on the streets as did the bustle of muted men and women. Children, dirty-faced and quick as foxes, darted from shadowy corners to engage in a type of hunt-and-be-hunted game with each other before disappearing again.

Suddenly, the carriage jerked to a halt, and Violet lurched

forward. The young coachman stood up in his box seat and shouted, gesturing with his hands at whatever obstructed his path.

It must be a stray, Violet thought, and turned back to the window. A pair of wanting eyes peered at her from behind the glass, and then face of a small girl came into view. Violet drew in her breath. The child raised her cupped hands toward the window just as the carriage propelled forward.

Violet's insides trembled. Why did she accept her aunt's invitation to come to this clattering, foul-smelling city that turned governesses into harlots and children into strays? Had grief for her papa driven her mad?

No—not mad—desperate. She'd become little more than a servant in her former home after Papa's death—forced to spend her days chasing after the new vicar's daughters, overseeing their tedious sewing samples, and teaching them how to read. When Papa died, she lost everything, including her freedom. Her aunt's invitation had come as a welcome surprise, so she'd avoided thinking about the motives behind it.

It wasn't long before the landscape changed. The streets appeared cleaner, the neighborhoods greener, and the houses grander. Women with coiffed hair wore wide, colorful dresses and fancy hats. And suited gentlemen traversed the pavements with expensive-looking walking canes. It pleased Violet to see cherub-faced, well-dressed children skipping alongside their caretakers.

Although relieved to be away from the distressing hints of poverty that punctuated the city, the finery of this neighborhood unnerved Violet. She did not belong in such an environment— that much would be obvious to anyone who met her. Then a thought dawned on her that made her grow cold. Did her aunt intend to position her as a servant in her household? No doubt, she thought that nobler than letting her sister's sole surviving child remain a paid drudge under the very roof that she had once called her own.

The carriage rolled to a stop in front of a row of stately homes. The coachman hopped down, opened the carriage door, and announced, "Astyr residence."

Violet reached for her carpetbag and allowed the coachman to assist her as she stepped out of the carriage. She blinked at the grand home, which stretched three stories high. Its pristine white exterior, adorned with sash windows and an arched entryway secured by Greek columns, seemed to highlight her plainness and made her want to shrink and disappear.

But she was afforded no such luxury. Instead, she squared her shoulders and raised her head. She was indeed a poor relation, but she would waste no time letting her aunt know that she neither wanted nor expected charity.

St. James's Independent School for Boys, London

BYRON THOMAS STOOD watching out the arched window that overlooked the school's stone courtyard. Chapel had ended, and the sixth-form boys lingered in the quad. They stood with their hands in their trouser pockets, talking and laughing together, looking at ease in their tailcoats and top hats like the little lords of a mini kingdom.

A younger lad—one of the new students who didn't yet understand the need to steer clear of the sixth-form monarchs—suddenly dashed across the courtyard, red-faced and carrying a load of books under his arm. Byron shook his head in sympathy for the poor lad as one of the sixth formers casually slid his foot into the boy's path. The child thudded onto the stone, his hat bouncing off his head and his books scattering. The older boys roared, laughing and clapping as if the court jester had just fallen down for their amusement. He sighed as he watched the lad struggle to his feet. *You'd best keep a stiff upper lip, Laddie. Gather your things and keep moving as if nothing happened.*

Byron turned away then to stare at the pile of ink-blotted notebooks on his desk. There was no doubt. He could not face correcting another error-laden Latin translation, and his short reprieve at the window hadn't helped to improve his mood. His father's harsh criticism plagued his thoughts. *Did I pay for you to attend Cambridge and obtain triposes in mathematics and the classics, all so you could spend your life correcting crude translations produced by the spoilt sons of the upper class? To what end?*

More than ten years had passed since he'd last laid eyes on his father, yet the man's memory still gave rise to a wave of bitter anger. That cruel bastard had chased his mother into an early grave and forced him to live in terror for much of his childhood. He had long since resolved never to see his father again, so why could he not erase his hateful words from his memory?

Byron's head throbbed, and he squeezed the bridge of his nose, attempting to alleviate the pain. He must look to the future and forget the past. His father was an ignorant bully. Byron knew full well that his work involved more than teaching lads to parrot the Greats. He was responsible for shaping minds and characters—for making men out of boys. And if his relationship with the headmaster's daughter blossomed, he might very well take over that coveted position one day.

"Sir?" Henry Phillips, one of the sixth-form prefects, stood in the doorway of the teaching auditorium.

"Yes, Phillips. What is it?"

"Headmaster Briggs requires your presence in his office, sir."

"Now?" He reached for his pocket watch, speaking more to himself than to Phillips.

"Yes, sir."

It was almost 9 o'clock, and his lesson would commence in ten minutes. Byron went to retrieve his mortarboard, certain this "urgent" meeting wasn't urgent at all but had something to do with the headmaster's wife and her ladies' college, where he'd been giving occasional evening lectures on Greek Mythology since the start of the year. His lectures had proven so popular that the headmistress had asked him to devise and teach a course of study in the classics. He'd been skeptical of the arrangement at first, as he was already engaged full-time at St. James's, but when he'd learned the headmaster himself was to cover his duties while he taught the ladies, he could hardly refuse.

"You will remain here and monitor the boys until I return," Byron said, turning back to Phillips.

"Of course, sir."

"They are to redo those translations from Virgil's *Aeneid*." He gestured to the pile of notebooks. "And mind they do better this time."

"Yes, sir." Tall and self-assured, Phillips stalked to the schoolmaster's table and curled his lip into a sneer upon glancing at the translations.

The boy's condescension gave Byron pause. He wondered who Phillips had learned it from—the other boys, one of his schoolmasters, or his father? How many of these lads were destined to become tyrants after suffering the tyranny of a brutal father?

"Phillips," he said.

"Sir?"

"Use the cane sparingly. You are too free with that thing."

The boy furrowed his brows in apparent disappointment. "But sir—"

"A bully with permission to be in charge is still only a bully, Phillips. Remember that."

Without waiting for a reply, Byron exited the auditorium and made his way along the stone corridors to the headmaster's office. As he walked, he smiled at the prospect ahead of him. Lecturing weekly at the ladies' college would help reduce the tedium of his current routine. And the headmaster was sure to allow him plenty of leeway as he ferried between the school and the college. His spirits soared at the thought, and he arrived at the headmaster's office in a cheerful mood.

Then it dawned on him. He knew why the headmaster wanted to see him. And he groaned inwardly.

CHAPTER TWO

*There is a worse evil under the sun, and that is–a female
Poor Relation.*

—Charles Lamb, *Poor Relations*

VIOLET STOOD IN front of the blue door and took a deep
breath before gripping the brass knocker and tapping it
twice. Her heart echoed the short sharp raps as she waited for a
response. Would she recognize her aunt after all these years?
Would her aunt recognize her? And what about her Uncle
Richard? Had Aunt Prudence warned him about her impending
arrival on his doorstep? If so, how had she obtained his permission?

She glanced over her shoulder toward the lower stairs that
led to the servants' entrance. Her uncle had never liked Violet's
mother or her family. She'd heard Mama and Aunt quarreling
about it once. Uncle Richard thought Papa poor, Dartmoor
backward, Frances and Sebastian wild, and Violet peculiar. She
still remembered the sting of those words.

The door creaked and a voice drawled, "May I help you?"

Violet jumped and turned to see a sour-faced butler addressing her from a small crack in the doorway.

She straightened her back, hoping to look more confident
than she felt. "Miss Violet Greyson to see Lady Astyr."

The butler did not budge and continued to guard the doorway as though Queen Victoria herself were in residence.

"Miss Greyson, did you say?" He narrowed his eyes, giving Violet the impression that he sought to mine her brain for nuggets of deceit.

"That is correct." Violet's confidence started to wane, and her throat went dry. "I am Lady Astyr's niece, come from Dartmoor. She is expecting me."

The butler relaxed his stance. "Indeed, she is waiting for you in the drawing room." He widened the opening and moved aside to let Violet enter. She stepped into an elegant hallway decorated in blue and gold and plastered with gilded-framed paintings.

"Follow me. You may leave your luggage here. It will be taken to your room for your convenience."

My room, Violet thought. *How odd that sounds.*

The butler set off across an exquisite Persian rug that ran from the entrance hall up the length of the stairs.

Violet took a step forward and then hesitated. "Shall I take off my shoes?" she asked.

The butler stopped and turned to face her. "Your shoes, miss?"

She nodded, but the look of incredulity on the butler's face told her that she'd asked a ridiculous question.

"Certainly not, Miss," he said and then proceeded to walk up the stairs.

Violet frowned. Where was he going? He said that her aunt awaited her in the drawing room, so why was he taking her upstairs? Perhaps, she'd misunderstood, and he meant to show her to her bedroom first. Then why leave her carpetbag? Perhaps she should pick it up and bring it with her. It seemed ridiculous to leave it for someone else when she could carry it herself.

The butler stopped, evidently sensing that Violet wasn't behind him. He turned once again to address her, "Is something wrong, miss?"

Violet glanced at her carpetbag and then back at the butler, who stared at her in stony silence.

She shook her head.

"Are you ready to proceed to the drawing room?"

"Yes, thank you." Violet lifted her chin and strode forward to join the butler on the stairs. As she walked, her eyes traced the gold stems, leaves, and petals that formed a pattern on the blue-papered walls. It continued on the first floor, where, to Violet's surprise, the butler led her to the drawing room.

"Miss Greyson to see Lady Astyr."

The same dark blue and gold floral wallpaper flowed from the hallway onto the walls of the spacious drawing room. Gold-colored drapes complemented the wallpaper and hung parted from the windows to allow for light. A navy-blue settee and several curvaceous chairs of various sizes, all upholstered in the same color with tufted velvet, formed a semicircle in the center of the room. In one of these chairs, an older and plumper version of Violet's mother lowered her newspaper, removed her spectacles, and blinked at Violet.

She doesn't recognize me. Violet shifted uneasily on her feet, itching to turn and run.

"Oh, you poor dear!" Her aunt pushed herself out of her chair and opened her arms to welcome her niece. "Come and give your Aunt Prudence a hug."

This unexpected display of affection rendered Violet immobile.

Undeterred, Aunt Prudence swished forward in her purple taffeta skirt and encircled Violet in a warm embrace. Violet stiffened, but her aunt only tightened her grip. She tried to relax and enjoy the sensation of sinking against her aunt's matronly body. After all, the woman shared her mother's blood and was the closest Violet would ever come to embracing her dear mama again.

"Look at you!" Aunt Prudence stepped back and held Violet at arm's length. "So thin and pale." She shook her head. "And still so very plain. I'd hoped you would turn out a little more like your mama. Your dear sister Frances looked just like her, remember? She inherited my sister's beautiful, dark curls and fine cheekbones."

Violet struggled against the old pain that lurked within the crevices of her heart. "Yes, Frances would have been a beautiful young lady, just like Mama."

"You take after your father, I'm afraid." Aunt Prudence pursed her lips in obvious disapproval. "What a pity."

"I am sorry if I disappoint you, Aunt." An edge of bitterness crept into Violet's tone, but her aunt didn't seem to notice.

"Do not fret. All is not lost. You have your mother's beautiful eyes—as light and blue as a cloudless sky. Your complexion is lovely too, my dear. You are very pale, to be sure, but your skin is creamy and smooth. After a good night's sleep, a new hairstyle, and a change of dress, you will be quite agreeable, I think."

Violet frowned. Her aunt talked about her as though she were a filly to be paraded at auction. "You forget that I wear black because I'm in mourning for my papa."

"Oh, my poor sister! Married to a penniless clergyman and forced to live like a peasant on those damp moorlands. What a harsh life she chose for herself!" Aunt Prudence's eyes watered. "In the end, it was all too much for her to bear, and she succumbed to it, poor dear."

"Consumption took Mama's life, just as it has taken thousands of other lives, rich and poor alike." Violet's voice sounded tight even to her own ears.

"A forbidding place, Dartmoor," Aunt Prudence continued without acknowledging Violet's words. "Uncultivated and austere. It killed your mother, and now, it has taken your father from you, too."

Violet closed her eyes and absorbed the fresh sting of her father's death. After a year, the pain still felt raw. "Oh, why do I prattle on so," Aunt Prudence chided herself and ushered Violet into a chair. "Come and sit. You must be starving after your long journey. Let me ring for tea." She reached for a small silver bell and gave it a quick shake before sitting down.

"Yes, my lady?" A servant girl appeared in the doorway as though she were an actress who had been waiting in the wings for her cue.

"Tea, Sara."

"Right away, my lady." The girl disappeared as quickly as she had appeared.

"I am sorry I took so long to send for you, my dear," Aunt Prudence said. "But I needed to wait for the right time, you see."

"The right time?"

Aunt Prudence paused. "I wanted to wait until Sir Richard departed for his trip to India."

"Why?" Violet asked before the realization dawned on her. "Oh, Aunt! You did not tell him about my coming here! Why didn't you ask his permission before inviting me?"

Aunt Prudence averted her gaze and fiddled with the napkin on her lap.

"Aunt Prudence?" Violet pressed.

"Sir Richard never did approve of my sister and her little family." The wrinkle between Aunt Prudence's brows deepened. "Especially after Elizabeth's and Frances's deaths, when Sebastian started giving your father all that trouble—" Her voice faltered. "That poor, dear boy. I should have done more for him."

An old, familiar pain reared inside Violet and stampeded through her with such force that she clutched at her stomach.

"Is that why you stopped writing and visiting us? Because Sir Richard forbade you?"

Aunt Prudence nodded. "After your mama died, Sir Richard ordered me to keep my distance. He stopped me from visiting, but he could not stop me from writing. Each time your father replied to one of my letters, the news distressed me so much that I would wring my hands for days. I'd hoped Sebastian would settle down after he accepted Frances's death, but he never did. The older he got, the wilder he became." Tears pooled in her eyes, and she dabbed at them with her handkerchief. "Sir Richard worried for my health, you see, so he forbade me to continue writing to your father. Every time a letter came from Devonshire, your uncle intercepted it. Eventually, the letters stopped coming."

"Oh, Aunt, I am sorry."

"We did not hear from your father again until—" She broke off her words. "Until Sebastian ran away from home. Your father came to London to look for him."

"I remember," Violet said.

"He arrived at the house unannounced and begged for my help. I, in turn, pleaded with your uncle to use his connections to find Sebastian. At first, he could find nothing of the boy, and then—" Aunt Prudence's shoulders sagged. She shook her head. "And then—well, your uncle received word that Sebastian bought passage to America on a ship called *The Oceanus*. And—well, you know the rest." Fresh tears pooled in her eyes.

Violet nodded. She remembered the day that fateful letter arrived at the vicarage. Papa stared at the envelope as if he could not believe news of his son had finally arrived. Then his hands began to tremble, and he tore the envelope open like a man dying of thirst. Violet watched as he devoured its contents. Then his eyes turned glassy, and his whole body sagged. He dropped the letter and retreated to his study without saying a word to Violet. She picked it up, and its terrible words imprinted themselves on her brain:

I regret to inform you that your son, Sebastian John Greyson, is listed as having bought passage on The Oceanus Steamship, which sank on July 7, 1856, while en route to America. There are no reported survivors.

Violet squeezed her eyes shut and concentrated on beating down and burying her pain, as she'd trained herself to do years ago.

Aunt Prudence dabbed at her tears. "I cried for days. It infuriated Sir Richard. He refused to allow me to contact you or your father because of my frail health. But I never forgot about you, Violet. I simply waited for the right time to send for you. Sir Richard is in India and will not be back for months."

"But he will return, and then he will be furious with you. I do not wish to cause any trouble."

"Do not worry about Sir Richard," Aunt Prudence said. "I shall sway him in our favor. He spends most of his time in India these days, so at the very least, he cannot begrudge me a companion."

Violet fell silent. Loneliness—that's what had prompted her aunt to send for her. At least being a Lady's companion was better than being a scullery maid. It was even better than being a governess because it might afford her some leisure time to read. But she could not accept payment for giving her aunt companionship, so she would still be living off her charity. And when her uncle returned from India—she shuddered at the memory of the disparaging glances he'd cast about at Mama's and Frances's funeral.

"I cannot—" she blurted, but stopped when Sara reentered the room, carrying a small tea tray filled with an array of delicacies. She placed the tray on the rectangular rosewood table that stood between Violet's and Aunt Prudence's chairs and poured two cups of tea. Then she retreated.

Violet reached for a custard-filled sponge cake coated with powdered sugar. Its creamy sweetness tasted luxurious and far richer than the scones served for tea at home. Despite her hunger, she could manage only a few bites before setting it aside in favor of her tea. The warmth of the liquid and the familiarity of the taste comforted her and helped to steady her nerves.

"Aunt Prudence, I want you to know that I am grateful for your kindness, but I am afraid I cannot accept charity and stay with you indefinitely. You see, I have plans of my own."

"What are you saying, dear girl?" She reached for Violet's hand and spoke in a low voice as though someone might overhear a terrible secret. "Do not tell me you have attached yourself to some country peasant."

Violet's skin prickled. "No, Aunt. I am not attached to anyone. I only mean that I do not intend to burden you or my uncle with the shame of a poor relation."

"No one need know you are poor, my dear. A few new dresses will transform you, and my lady's maid, Elsie, does wonders with hair."

Violet sighed, perturbed that her aunt who had ignored her for years, now wanted to turn her into a pet. "I cannot stay here, Aunt. By your own admittance, Sir Richard disapproves of my papa and our family."

"Sir Richard has some peculiar ways, but he is a good man at heart. I am certain he will—"

"No, Aunt." She shrank back. "I cannot."

"Then I will endeavor to find you a suitable match before he returns. I believe I know some elderly gentlemen desperate for heirs who will settle for a well-acquainted lady without a fortune. After all, I have no children of my own, and a grandnephew would be a blessing." She sniffed.

"Perhaps I am too proud, but I feel that I must make my own way in this world. I must work and pay for my own keep. If you wish to help me secure suitable employment, I would be most grateful."

Aunt Prudence stared at Violet in frozen silence. Then she blinked as if rescued from a horrible vision. "Employment? I don't understand. Do you object to marriage?"

"If I were to meet someone one day and fall in love, then I would have no objection to getting married. But I will not marry for security or convenience."

"Marrying for love is what your mother did, my child, and it killed her."

Violet pressed her lips together. "Mama was happy. She loved my father very much."

Clearly rattled, Aunt Prudence reached for the teapot and poured some fresh tea into her cup.

"You always were a strange girl." She stared reprovingly at Violet and, in doing so, overfilled her cup. The tea spilled into the saucer, ran over onto the table, and flowed onto the Persian rug.

Violet sprang from her seat and snatched the newspaper that lay on the table. "Here, let me help," she said, ready to lay down the paper and soak up the liquid.

"Sit down!" Aunt Prudence snapped. "That's a job for Sara, not you." She picked up the silver bell and shook it furiously.

Violet reclaimed her seat, still clutching the paper.

Sara reappeared at the door and, seeing the mess, hurried inside. Somewhat ashamed that she sat idly watching, as Sara cleaned and her aunt barked orders, Violet turned to the newspaper on her lap. She scanned the page without much interest until the words *Ladies' College* caught her eye. She blinked deliberately, certain that her exhausted mind was playing tricks on her. But the words were still there when she opened her eyes.

Wanted

Pupil-teacher to Classics Master at Westminster Ladies' College, London

Westminster Ladies' College in Pimlico is dedicated to expanding educational opportunities for women. We provide secondary and upper education to young ladies aged sixteen and above and award certificates of knowledge in several areas of study. Our lectures are conducted by visiting university professors and/or public schoolmasters who hold university degrees.

We are currently seeking an intelligent young lady who wishes to further her education and serve as pupil-teacher for our classic's master.

Strong reading, writing, and grammatical skills are required.

Some knowledge of the classics is necessary.

Compensation: Board and lodging, tuition, and a monthly stipend.

Ladies only.

Violet reread the advertisement twice to make sure she hadn't imagined the words. It appeared she had not: The advertisement was real. She smiled to herself. Her Papa had always said that God works in mysterious ways. She'd questioned that in the past, but now she wondered if it were true.

Violet waited for Sara to finish cleaning and leave the room before handing the newspaper to her aunt. "I think that I have found the answer to my prayers."

Aunt Prudence frowned. "In the *Times*?" She took the newspaper, and Violet stood up to point out the advertisement—one in a sea of many—vying for attention on the page.

Aunt Prudence put on her spectacles and furrowed her brow as she read.

"A Ladies' College?" she said, turning her attention from the page to Violet. "Do you wish to work at a school?"

"It's not a school for children, Aunt. It's for young ladies and not an ordinary one at that. It requires the candidate to have some knowledge of the classics."

Aunt Prudence's frown deepened. "What do you know of the classics?" she asked, eyeing the newspaper as though it were a slug that had taken up residence on her lap. "Headmistress Briggs," she read and lowered the newspaper. "Briggs," she muttered. "I know that name. I have heard of a Mrs. Briggs in Belgravia. She is a bluestocking and a radical of the worst kind." She held the newspaper out to Violet with a look of distaste.

"By radical, do you mean she fights against injustice and wants change?" Violet accepted the newspaper from her aunt and returned to her chair.

Aunt Prudence shifted in her seat, picked up her fresh tea, and took a sip. As though her confidence in the world had been restored by the tea, she reached across the table and patted Violet's hand. "You're tired and overexcited from your journey, my dear. Finish your tea and get a good night's rest. All will be well in the morning."

HEADMASTER BRIGGS SAT behind his polished mahogany desk, strategically placed in front of a large, mullioned window that overlooked the quad. "I want to thank you for everything you are doing to help make the Ladies' College successful, Thomas. The school means a great deal to Headmistress Briggs. She used her own fortune to fund it."

"I know, sir, and I admire her for it."

"I hope it won't be too much of a bother for you to go back and forth between St. James's and the Ladies' College. Of course, the school will pay for your cabs if necessary."

"Perhaps during the winter months. I welcome a good walk in the warmer months, especially when it involves crossing my favorite park."

Headmaster Briggs leaned back in his buttoned leather chair. "That's very gracious of you, but Headmistress Briggs wishes you would at least accept a stipend for your trouble."

"That's not necessary, sir. With you covering my duties here, I won't be losing any of my wages."

That is true, however—"

"Don't mention it again, or I shall decline the position." Byron held up his hand in protest.

He was adamant on this point. He'd accepted the position in part to honor the memory of his beloved Olivia and their sweet babe, who had not had the chance to blossom into a young lady or learn anything. But he did not articulate as much to the headmaster.

"I am honored Headmistress Briggs invited me to lecture at her college, truly. As you know, I am amongst those few who advocate for equality in education."

"As am I, Thomas. I truly believe in my wife's cause. But you are correct in saying we are in the minority. People call Mrs. Briggs a *radical*. And would you believe she enjoys the label?" He chuckled.

"Anyone who desires change and challenges long-held conventions is labeled a radical."

"Well said. That is exactly why Headmistress Briggs thinks so highly of you." Headmaster Briggs leaned his forearms on his desk and looked directly at Byron. "She's particularly excited about the course of lectures you'll be giving. It's controversial, but, like you and I, she knows that incorporating the classics is a key step in the direction of equal education, and nothing is more important to her than that."

"We are all in agreement, then." Byron wondered when the headmaster would get to the real point of this conversation.

The headmaster cleared his throat. "Headmistress Briggs is worried that you will become bogged down with the minutiae of things. She doesn't want to occupy more of your time than necessary."

Byron smiled, knowing they had reached the crux of the conversation. "She is concerned I have not yet appointed a pupil-teacher to assist me." Confident that he was correct, he framed his words as a statement rather than a question.

Headmaster Briggs raised his eyebrows. "Why haven't you? Your lectures are to begin next week. There must be one young lady who—"

"Indeed, there is. Unfortunately, the mathematics lecturer and I selected the same candidate."

"Ah, yes, Miss Hamilton. Headmistress Briggs tells me that she is exceptionally bright. Her father is a distinguished mathematician, you know, so I think she is well-placed. Did you not encounter any other promising students?"

Byron sighed. "I fear it will take more time and effort to train one of the other girls than to do things myself."

"Well, we must have someone. Headmistress Briggs wants her most promising students to be nurtured and trained as potential educators. She believes they are the school's future. It's an important part of her program. Is there not one candidate who stands out over the others?"

Byron paused and thought back to his interviews. In truth, he could not make a distinction between any of the young ladies he'd spoken to. He shifted in his seat.

"Why not revisit your notes this evening and narrow your choices?" Headmaster Briggs suggested. "Then you can make some further observations during the first week of lectures before finalizing your decision."

Byron nodded. Thankful the headmaster had given him a week's reprieve. He enjoyed lecturing at the Ladies' College, but the idea of taking a young lady under his wing didn't appeal to him. Unless already extremely capable, efficient, and knowledgeable, a pupil-teacher would be more of a hindrance than a help.

"But I must caution you." Headmaster Briggs pushed himself up from his chair. "If you do not act, Headmistress Briggs will likely choose for you." He walked around his desk to where Byron stood. "Now, can I count on you to dine with us on Sunday evening? I am certain Amelia will want to see you after her sojourn in France."

"Of course, sir." Byron eyed the paneled walls lined with portraits of headmasters dating back to the seventeenth century and reminded himself that a successful courtship of the headmaster's stepdaughter meant this office could one day belong to him.

CHAPTER THREE

Behold!—The world of books is still the world!
—Elizabeth Barrett Browning, *Aurora Leigh*

Westminster Ladies' College, London

THE CLASSICS MASTER appraised Violet with a long and silent stare, but his composed countenance gave none of his thoughts away. She, in turn, eyed the starched white collar and pressed black suit that peeked out from under his intimidating scholarly robes and the unyielding mortarboard that crowned his head. She understood how she must look to his eyes—homely, unsophisticated, and insignificant—standing before him in her crude mourning dress and country bonnet. He likely wondered whether she knew the difference between Homer and Virgil and questioned what business she had applying for a position at an establishment as excellent as Westminster Ladies' College. The thought both terrified and angered her.

In a show of defiance and feigned confidence, she lifted her chin and met his eyes. But her bravado immediately faltered. She'd expected his eyes to be austere and inflexible, matching his aquiline nose and rigid jawline. Instead, they were soulful, hazel in color, and flecked with specks of gold.

They were the eyes of a poet, not those of an unbending

master.

"A pleasure to meet you, Miss Greyson." His voice, smooth and confident, brought her back to reality.

She returned his greeting with a curt, "Sir." But her voice came out in a half-whisper, and it made her want to kick herself.

The corners of the master's mouth edged upward, and Violet could not tell if his smile was due to amusement or arrogance. She decided upon the latter.

"Thank you again for coming at such short notice, Mr. Thomas." Headmistress Briggs rose from her desk. "I think you will find it to be worth your while. I simply could not let Miss Greyson leave without seeing you."

"Of course, Headmistress. Are we ready to begin?"

"Please, use my chair while you conduct your interview. I left notes on my desk for your reference. I will stay in the capacity of a chaperone. But this is your interview, so pretend I am not here."

Mr. Thomas seated himself behind the desk and scanned the headmistress's notes set out in front of him. Violet straightened her shoulders and concentrated on steeling her nerves. She needed to impress this gentleman. Headmistress Briggs had explained that although she owned the college, she relied on male scholars to teach the secondary-level courses. Women could not attend university, and only very few held a secondary education. Those who did were required to serve as tutors until the headmistress deemed them ready to teach. In light of that, Violet knew it would be the classics master, not Headmistress Briggs, who ultimately decided her fate.

Mr. Thomas looked up from the notes. "I see that you are recently arrived in London from Devonshire. What brought you here?"

"The death of my father, sir," she said. "It rendered me an orphan. I found work as a governess in Dartmoor—" she swallowed—"but the memories were too painful, so I decided to come to London. That is when I saw your advertisement."

He eyed her somber dress and frowned. "Are you currently in deep mourning?"

"Not officially. My father died a little over a year ago, but I still feel his death keenly."

He nodded. "And what attracted you to Westminster Ladies' College? Do you wish to improve your skills as a governess and earn a certificate to help you obtain a better job in London? These days, many families favor governesses who hold certificates, but you certainly can find a position without one if you have the right connections."

"I do not wish to continue working as a governess—that is—if I can avoid it."

"Do you wish to earn a teaching certificate, then?" There are several training colleges that can prepare you for a position as a primary teacher."

"I have no interest in attending a training college or teaching in a primary school."

"Then tell me your purpose, Miss Greyson."

I came here because I want to learn."

"To what end?"

"Because my brain craves it—demands it, even. I hate for my mind to be idle, and I want to engage with like-minded people."

"Very good, Miss Greyson. Very good, indeed."

Violet's heart leapt. Finally, he seemed pleased with her answer.

"A few more questions," he said and glanced once more at the headmistress's notes. "I understand that your father was a vicar, correct?"

"Yes, that is correct."

"Were you sent to a parish school as a child?"

"No, my father elected to teach me at home."

"I see," he said in a tone that worried Violet. "You are well-versed in the Bible, no doubt?"

"Certainly."

"Church of England?"

"Yes."

He folded his hands together on the desk and looked intently at Violet. "You are aware that Westminster Ladies' College does not cater to one particular denomination, are you not?"

"I am not sure what you mean," Violet said.

"I mean, this school doesn't identify as an Anglican institution per se."

Violet blinked, uncertain how to respond.

"In other words, the majority of our young ladies are nonconformists."

"Dissenters?"

"Exactly."

Violet swallowed as she envisioned her father turning over in his grave.

The classics master watched her closely. "If this institution doesn't best suit your needs there are others—"

Violet saw opportunity slipping away. "It suits my needs perfectly," she interrupted. "I am here to obtain an academic education, not a religious one, so I do not imagine that the religious affiliations of others will be of any concern to me."

"That is all very well but given that you were raised in a strictly Anglican home and educated solely by your minister father, I wonder how well-equipped you are to serve as my assistant."

Violet swallowed the lump of anger that rose in her throat. The man's assumptions were insufferable. "I am very well equipped for it," she said, her confidence returning as she sensed the opportunity to convey her strengths. "I am sorry if I gave you the impression that I read only the Bible growing up. I can assure you that reading materials of all types have been my constant companions since I was a little girl. Indeed, every thrill I have ever experienced and every bit of adventure I have ever encountered has come from reading."

He scoffed. "I am talking about literature, Miss Greyson, not the penny dreadfuls."

A searing heat rose in Violet's chest and spread from her neck and her cheeks. She opened her mouth to speak but closed it again, fearing that she could not defend herself and remain polite.

⫸⫷

MISS GREYSON'S ALABASTER skin flushed red, and Byron knew from the stony expression on her face that anger and not shame caused her to color. He smiled inwardly. *She has a strong spirit. Now let her show it.*

"Well, Miss Greyson? Can you enlighten me further as to your abilities to assist me in the classroom? Be specific."

She squared her frame and glared at him through blue eyes that glistened with indignation. The rest of her petite features were partially obscured by her oversized black bonnet, making her look like a vexed tomcat. "My father taught me to value *literature*, not sensationalism, Mr. Thomas. We spent many an hour discussing the works of Bunyan, Milton, and Dante. Those authors were amongst his favorites."

"And what of your favorites?" Byron asked, curious to know more.

"On my own, I indulged in the poetry of Byron—Childe Harold being my favorite—Shelley, Wordsworth, Keats, Coleridge, and Tennyson, of course. Of novelists, Thackeray remains my favorite, but I have loved Defoe's Crusoe and Swift's Gulliver since I was a child.

"Thackeray and Swift? You are an admirer of satire, then?"

"I'm an admirer of good writing."

"And what of the Greeks? How well versed are you in Greek mythology?

"I know the gods—the Olympians—and a few others I gleaned from reading snatches of Ovid's poetry, more from Shakespeare, and a good deal from Homer."

"*The Odyssey?*"

"I have read both *The Iliad* and *The Odyssey* more than once.

They have always delighted me."

"The *Iliad*?" Byron found himself doubting her now. "Do you mean that your father read parts of it to you?"

"No, I do not."

"Then, are you saying that your father told you the story in his own words?"

She looked at him pointedly. "I am saying that I read it in its entirety on my own, more than once."

"How unusual. I've decided against it for the lectures. I do not imagine that even the daughters of radicals will have the interest or the stomach for it."

"I beg to differ, sir," she burst out and then shrank back as if realizing her folly.

"And why is that?"

"Because it's brimming with passion and pathos, gods and heroes, love and war, self-sacrifice and hubris. How could anyone not appreciate such richness and beauty?" Her alabaster skin, which had made her seem rather meek when she first entered the room, now glowed as though Homer's epic lit her up from the inside.

Byron studied her. He found her enthusiasm enchanting, and he sensed there was a lot more to learn about this unique young woman sitting before him. "Where came you upon all these texts? Did your father keep an extensive library?"

"Not an extensive one, but he owned a good selection of books from his days at Oxford, and he added to it every year."

"Oxford." Byron scanned the notes for confirmation.

"He attended on scholarship," she added as though suspecting he doubted her word. "My mother also kept a small collection of novels—"

"Did your father teach you any Latin or Greek?"

She hesitated and, for the first time during the interview, averted her eyes while answering him. "I know a little of both languages. But I fare better with Greek."

Byron intertwined his fingers and surveyed her. She appeared to be omitting some truth.

"You have practiced translating passages from Homer?"

She looked up. "Yes, many times. I provided Headmistress Briggs with a few samples of my work, but I can attempt a translation now if you wish."

Byron glanced at the headmistress, who nodded her affirmation.

"That will not be necessary. The samples you gave Headmistress Briggs will suffice." Byron settled back in his chair without taking his eyes off Miss Greyson, who now seemed the furthest thing in the world from the unremarkable country girl he'd mistaken her for.

CHAPTER FOUR

So you judge!
Because I love the beautiful, I must
Love pleasure chiefly, and be overcharged
For ease and whiteness!
—Elizabeth Barrett Browning, *Aurora Leigh*

*P*ENNY DREADFULS, INDEED!

Mr. Thomas's words loitered in Violet's head. She paced the brick pathway outside the college without stopping to admire the purple pansies and yellow daffodils that lined it on either side. Did he presume all women were inherently empty-headed and so preferred to entertain themselves by reading sensationalist nonsense? To be sure, he would not have suggested such a thing to a male candidate.

I am talking about literature, Miss Greyson, not the penny dreadfuls! Perhaps it was just her he thought ignorant—and not all women. She remembered his initial silent appraisal of her. No doubt, he had dismissed her as a simple country girl at first sight. The thought simmered in her stomach. Well, she had done her part to prove him wrong! He had been pompous and rude, and she had held her own and prevailed. For each of his questions, she had provided a solid answer. She knew that her reading accomplishments and her knowledge of the classics were impressive.

How many young ladies could translate ancient Greek? She bit her lip. No doubt many at a place like this. Mr. Thomas most likely had an excellent pool of candidates from which to choose an assistant—girls educated by open-minded fathers and bluestocking mothers.

Violet did not know what to make of the jumble of emotions inside her. On the one hand, she desperately wanted Mr. Thomas's approval. She craved the opportunity to assist him in the classroom and to learn from him. On the other hand, his air of smug superiority infuriated her.

Her eyes scaled the length of the red brick building before her and located the window to the headmistress's office, identifying it by the forest-green drapes that framed its sides. She searched for signs of movement but could detect none. At the conclusion of the interview, Headmistress Briggs had requested that she wait outside and suggested she take a stroll in the garden. Violet thought this encouraging at first, but now she was starting to worry. What were they talking about up there? Were they debating her suitability for the position? What if he was up there at this very moment, convincing Headmistress Briggs that she was not qualified for the position? What would she do if they turned her away? She did not want to be a governess who spent her days teaching little girls how to read and sew.

Violet pulled at the collar of her dress. The thought of returning to such a dull existence stifled her. Yet, it was a far better option than a loveless marriage. And marriage in itself was unlikely. She shuddered at the thought of spending her days imprisoned in a fancy house like Aunt Prudence, too frightened and powerless to do anything other than order the servants about. At least a spinster could come and go as she pleased and spend what she earned, no matter how small the sum. Violet sighed.

Here she stood, no less imprisoned than her aunt, waiting for a gentleman's approval and permission to move forward. Headmistress Briggs had already decided upon her, but that was no matter. The future she desired lay in the hands of the classics master, Byron Thomas.

"Is she not a marvel?" Headmistress Briggs beamed. "So well-read for such a young lady! It is my dream that all of England will one day be filled with well-educated and articulate young ladies like Miss Greyson."

"She appears to be tolerably intelligent," Byron said. The girl had surprised and intrigued him in many ways, but he hardly thought it appropriate to gush.

"Come now, Mr. Thomas. She is far more than tolerably intelligent. Miss Greyson is self-taught. Imagine how she will blossom under your tutelage. But more importantly, she has fire inside her and a true passion for learning. She is the type of woman I need within these walls." She gestured to the unassuming walls, papered in beige on top and trimmed with dark panels on the bottom. "The type we all need on our side," she continued, "if we are to succeed in the battle for the continued growth of women's education." She took two steps forward and peered out the window. "It takes bravado to go against the norms of society and fight for change."

A trace of bitterness rose in Byron's throat. He, too, had been full of bravado in his youth, but life had a cruel way of dousing one's fire.

Headmistress Briggs turned to face Byron. "What say you, Mr. Thomas? Will she make an acceptable assistant for you?"

Byron joined Headmistress Briggs by the window and looked down at the lush garden, enclosed at its edges by London Planes trees. The petite figure of Miss Greyson, dressed in black from head to toe, paced back and forth on the brick pathway that led from the college entrance to the college gate. He frowned and rubbed his chin. "Her knowledge of the classics is impressive, but

I fear the pupils will not relate well to her." He continued to watch Miss. Greyson's pacing figure. "Her mannerisms are unusual, and her dress is rather...quaint. I worry that the young ladies will fail to take her seriously." He straightened and folded his arms.

Headmistress Briggs nodded. "You make a valid point. And I have given some thought to that already. The students will undoubtedly judge her—as you call it—quaint appearance. It is a delicate matter, but I believe that my daughter can be of some assistance."

"Amelia?" Byron could not keep the shock out of his voice.

"She is only a few years younger than Miss Greyson, and I think some gentle advice from her will be well received. Amelia tires of her dresses rather quickly. Perhaps, with a few adjustments, she can nudge Miss Greyson toward a more modern wardrobe."

Byron blinked back his incredulity. Handing Miss Greyson over to Amelia would be akin to feeding a rabbit to a bloodhound. He wondered how Headmistress Briggs could be so blind to the reality of her own daughter's character. "Are you certain that Amelia—" he paused, wanting to choose his words carefully—"would enjoy such a task? Perhaps one of the pupil teachers is better suited to handle such a delicate matter. Miss Hamilton, for instance? As a peer, she will have a clearer understanding of the situation."

"I quite agree, and I certainly shall enlist Miss Hamilton's help in making Miss Greyson feel welcomed and comfortable at the school. But Miss Greyson will need more than one friend, and I want to encourage Amelia's participation in the college. Perhaps this small task will draw her a little closer to our cause."

"Has she expressed an interest in becoming involved?"

Headmistress Briggs gave a little shrug. "Not yet, but we shall see. She'll be back from France tomorrow, and judging from her letters home these past months, she finds everything French enthralling, so I hope to strike while the iron is hot and procure her services as a French tutor."

"Indeed," Byron said, although he doubted Amelia's enthusiasms for France extended beyond the latest fashions.

"At any rate, I am certain she will bring a chest full of dresses back from France, so I will ask her to sort through her wardrobe this weekend and pick out a few items for our Miss Greyson." She cocked her head. "Am I correct in affirming that you will be joining us for dinner at the house to welcome Amelia home?"

"Yes, Headmaster Briggs already extended the invitation. Thank you."

"Wonderful! Amelia will be anxious to see you, I am sure."

Byron nodded, but he wasn't so sure. His relationship with Amelia had been more of a flirtation than a courtship, and he hadn't received a letter from her while she'd been away. If he could only muster the enthusiasm to court Miss Farthington in earnest, then he'd have a better chance of securing the position of headmaster after her stepfather retired.

"Now, back to the matter at hand." Headmistress Briggs slapped her palms together as if to remind herself to get back on task. "If all goes well, I believe Miss Greyson will have a wonderful future at Westminster Ladies' College. What say you?"

Byron peered down at the figure of Miss Greyson, once again. She'd stopped pacing and now appeared to be inspecting something in the sky, using her hand to provide an extra layer of shade where her bonnet ended. She was undoubtedly more interesting and more promising than the other students he'd interviewed; still, he was reluctant to take on the responsibility of a pupil-teacher.

"It will be a shame to turn her away." The headmistress let out an exaggerated sigh. "But I must save the scholarships for the pupil teachers."

It certainly would be a shame to turn her away. Byron found himself silently agreeing with the headmistress.

"Well, in that case, I suppose it is the right thing to do, he said. "She certainly seems capable, so perhaps she will fare well under my instruction."

"Capable, indeed!" Headmistress Briggs chuckled, making it difficult to discern whether or not his response pleased or irritated her. "Mr. Thomas, I admire your reserve, but you know as well as I do that her talents stretch beyond mere capabilities. I want you to take great care with her instruction. Women like Miss Greyson are our future educators and will raise the standards for female education in England."

"I am sure you are correct," Byron said. "And I will do all I can to encourage Miss Greyson's studies and future at Westminster Ladies' College."

"Thank you, Mr. Thomas. I am already indebted to you for your wonderful contributions to our future. Now, I must detain you no longer. It's nearing two o'clock, and you have young men awaiting your instruction."

"To be sure," Byron said, surprised that the time had passed so quickly. Had he really spent almost two hours immersed in interviewing and discussing Miss Greyson? The previous interviews he'd conducted had ended swiftly, with the candidates promptly dismissed and forgotten after their departure.

"Mr. Thomas?" Headmistress Briggs interrupted his thoughts. "Why do you frown so? Is something wrong?"

"Not at all," he said. "I was only thinking about a matter that needed my attention. I must make haste and get back."

"Yes, do, or Headmaster Briggs will hold me accountable."

Byron tipped his mortarboard at the headmistress and hurried out of her office.

VIOLET WAS STILL trying to detect movement in the headmistress's office when Mr. Thomas stepped onto the pathway where she stood. She jerked her head around in surprise as he strode past her.

"Good day, Miss Greyson," he said without stopping.

She watched him go with a sinking heart. His words rang like a dismissal in her ears. What was she to do now? She turned to face the building's entrance, hoping to catch sight of the headmistress. Had all her efforts come to naught? She twisted her gloved hands. She could not bear to return prospectless to her aunt's house. Aunt Prudence would surely use it as an opportunity to start treating her like a doll to be dressed and combed. Violet's anxiety threatened to reach a crescendo when the door to the college opened, and Headmistress Briggs stepped outside. Violet had to restrain herself from running toward the woman as she descended the steps.

"Congratulations, Miss Greyson! You have cracked the uncrackable!" the headmistress said when she reached Violet.

Violet blinked, unable to process what the headmistress meant by her words.

"Are you not pleased?" Headmistress Briggs asked, evidently perplexed by Violet's expression.

"He approves of me, then? And he has chosen me for his assistant?"

"Of course, he has chosen you! How could he not? You are a marvel!"

"It is only that he seemed, well, rather unimpressed by me." Violet turned to peer in the direction in which he'd walked. Away. With barely a word or a hint of…anything. What an odd man, she thought.

"That is simply his way of doing things." Headmistress Briggs linked her arm in Violet's and led her across the garden. "Mr. Thomas has had the privilege of a Cambridge education and has been in the company of learned men all his life. Unlike you and I, and most women of our acquaintance, he has never been denied access to learning or forced to endure insipid conversations simply because of his sex, nor will he ever be able to comprehend what that entails."

As the headmistress spoke, Violet recalled the times she sat outside her father's study with her ear pressed to the door and her mouth moving in silent unison with Sebastian's as he recited the Greek alphabet out loud. How she'd longed to be permitted to learn with Sebastian, but Papa saw no merit in it. With no one to mother Sebastian, Violet had taken on that duty, and she could not afford to spend hours locked away in her father's study translating Greek and Latin verses. Her turn came late at night when Sebastian and her father slept. Then, Violet would complete Sebastian's translations for the following day's lesson. Papa never discovered their secret, or if he had, he never disclosed as much to Violet.

"You are very quiet, Miss Greyson. You really mustn't take Mr. Thomas's mannerisms to heart. Although I warrant, he can be a little abrupt at times."

Still prickling from the painful memory, she said, "I think accusing me of indulging in the penny dreadfuls was rather discourteous." She watched the words slip off her tongue and take the shape of a petulant child. Violet bit her lip. She hadn't meant to voice her thoughts out loud. Why could she not control her tongue?

"I believe he was merely testing your muster. You must understand that the future of women's education cannot be birthed, fully formed, like Athena from Zeus's head. Think of it, instead, in terms of real childbirth—a lengthy and painful process with a priceless reward at the end. Women like us are on an arduous journey, and we must have strong characters. Not only do we need to win men over to our thinking, but we must win women also. Many mothers worry that too much education will render their daughters unladylike, and some persist in their belief that learning is perilous to a woman's mental health."

"That is preposterous," Violet said.

"But true, nonetheless, and I think Mr. Thomas prefers to err on the side of caution in this matter. I rather liked that you extolled the virtues of *The Iliad*. Perhaps, over time, you can persuade him to incorporate it into his lectures."

"Do you truly believe that I might have the power to influence his thinking?"

"I do. Mr. Thomas is not a closed-minded man. He is intelligent and a progressive thinker. But he is also cautious, and you will have to gain his trust before you can sway his thinking."

Violet fell silent. Perhaps she had misjudged Mr. Thomas. She thought of the softness in his hazel eyes, and the memory brought a rising warmth to her chest.

"Does that suit you, Violet?"

Violet turned to the headmistress, who appeared to be waiting for an answer to a question.

"Yes, perfectly," Violet said, without knowing what she consented to.

"Wonderful! We dine at six. I will send a hansom for you at five o'clock on Sunday evening. My daughter Amelia has recently returned from France, and I would so like you to meet her."

Violet's head whirled. Had she just accepted an invitation to dine at the headmistress's home?

"Now, let's get you settled in your new room in the residence hall. Since you are a lecturer's assistant, you will have a private room. It is nothing grand, mind you, but it does have a small fireplace. And we provide house servants who will take care of your laundry needs and deliver water and towels for your morning wash. Classes begin on Wednesday morning, so you will have plenty of time to move in this weekend. Where are you staying now?"

"Oh, with friends; not far from here." After hearing Aunt Prudence's derogatory remarks about Headmistress Briggs, Violet decided that it was best not to mention her relative.

"Wonderful! I will give you a key for the main building and your room today. And then you can move in as soon as you wish."

"Thank you, Headmistress. You are too kind."

"It is not kindness that compels me, child. I want you for my school and my cause, and I am therefore prepared to invest in your future. So do not disappoint me."

Invest in your future. Violet turned the phrase over in her mind. It tasted sweet. Her father had spent years investing in her brother's future while assuming she'd safeguard hers by investing in a husband. Society deemed men a worthy investment, Violet thought. Men served their country in parliament, the military, or business. But what of women? If not a wife or a mother, what was she to society? A burden.

A fire ignited in Violet's chest. Suddenly, she wanted nothing more than to succeed, not only for herself but for Headmistress Briggs, the college, and all the women who wished to invest in their futures.

"I shan't disappoint," she said. "That, I promise you."

CHAPTER FIVE

I wandered lonely as a cloud
That floats on high o'ver vales and hills,
When all at once I saw a crowd,
A host of golden daffodils;
Beside the lake, beneath the trees,
Fluttering and dancing in the breeze
—Wordsworth, "I Wandered Lonely as a Cloud"

BYRON STROLLED ACROSS Green Park, pleased that he'd given himself ample time to enjoy spring's daffodils on his way to the Briggs's townhome in Belgravia. Walking in nature always helped clear his mind, and he desperately needed to do just that. A restlessness had plagued him these past few days, but he couldn't quite place the reason for his agitation. He suspected that it had something to do with Amelia's return from France. He didn't love her, and he knew she did not love him. But for reasons unclear to him, she'd been open to his courtship. Possibly because her mother's reputation as a radical had ruined her chances for a better match. He did not know, nor did he care. His one true love had died seven years ago, and he'd vowed never to venture down love's path again. He'd become reconciled to the idea of marrying Amelia because their marriage would ensure his place as the next headmaster of St. James's. However, now that it was time to commit fully to the courtship, he found himself reluctant to do so.

Byron slowed his pace and gazed at the oasis before him, the tension in his body slowly releasing as he took in nature's beauty. Thoughts of Amelia dissipated, and his mind wandered to Miss Greyson. She intrigued him, or rather, she aroused his curiosity. He hadn't expected such a small and unworldly woman—the daughter of a wasteland vicar—to possess so much passion and intelligence. She'd taken him by surprise, speaking with such passion and conviction in her defense of *The Iliad*.

Miss Greyson reminded him of his Olivia, who'd carried a similar fiery passion within her. Perhaps that's why he'd caught himself thinking about his new pupil-teacher on more than one occasion since their interview—even looking forward to their next meeting. He barely knew her, yet she'd awakened something in him—a stirring not felt since the death of his wife. It gave him a secret pleasure, but it also terrified him. He'd spent years deadening his emotions, and he had no desire to rekindle them.

By the time he reached the Briggs's elegant Georgian town-home some thirty minutes later, Byron's restlessness had ceased, and he was ready for a strong glass of port and a hearty meal. He stepped onto the portico in good spirits and rapped on the door.

Less than a minute later, the Briggs's butler, Collins, opened the door and greeted him with a smile. "Evening, Mr. Thomas."

"Collins." Byron stepped inside.

"They are waiting for you in the drawing room, sir."

Byron followed Collins and waited for him to announce his arrival before entering the drawing room.

"Thomas!" Mr. Briggs looked up from pouring his glass of port. "Care for a glass?" He held up the crystal decanter.

"Certainly," Byron said.

"How wonderful that you have come early," Mrs. Briggs said. "It will give us some time to talk before Miss Greyson arrives."

The announcement caught Byron off guard. He steadied himself, not wanting to reveal anything more than a casual interest. "Is Miss Greyson coming to dinner?"

"Yes. I want to make her feel as welcome as possible. She is new to London, and I am sure she doesn't have many friends. We discussed this, did we not?"

Byron nodded. "I remember. Forgive me."

Mr. Briggs made his way to Byron and handed him a glass of port. Byron thanked him and sipped his drink in silence, his mind on Miss Greyson.

"I do hope you are satisfied with Miss Greyson and don't feel she's been forced upon you," Mrs. Briggs said.

Her husband chuckled, "Of course she was forced upon him, my dear. You were quite determined that she was the best candidate."

"And I was right. Like Miss Hamilton, that young lady is a miracle."

The door to the drawing room opened. "Who's a miracle, Mama?" Amelia asked as she stepped inside.

Amelia looked striking in a crimson dress that curved around her shoulders, dipped daringly between her cleavage, and cinched her tiny waist. The vibrant red complemented her dark curls, which she wore swept back in some type of intricate French knot. She was even more exquisite than he remembered, but that is where her charm ended.

"Mr. Thomas's new assistant," Mrs. Briggs said in answer to Amelia's question. "She's extremely intelligent and most impressive."

"Is she also poor and ill-favored?" Amelia asked. Her large dark eyes smiled at Byron and sparkled with malice.

"Amelia!" her mother scolded.

"Mama, you know as well as I do that the only type of women who require intelligence are poor and ill-favored ones."

Byron sank into a chair and sighed inwardly.

"I taught you better than that!" Red splotches appeared on Mrs. Briggs's cheeks. "You know that I do not run a school of manners. I do not approve of grooming young ladies to become pretty ornaments in their husbands' homes. Nor did I raise you to be one. Have I spent my life fighting to further the education of women only to have my daughter scorn it?"

Amelia snorted and sat on the chair next to Byron. "Oh Mama, I am teasing you. You make it so easy for me to do so."

Mrs. Briggs settled into her chair. "Well, Amelia, if you do not believe all you have said, then you might take a greater interest in the college. We could use a talented French tutor."

"Teaching does not please me, Mama. I am not you, after all."

The door to the drawing room swung open, and Collins reappeared. "Miss Violet Greyson," he announced.

Byron and Mr. Briggs stood as Miss Greyson stepped out from behind Collins and into view. She looked as peculiar and out of place as she had when Byron first met her, wearing a simple, homemade, olive-green gown that did not match the fashion of the day. Nonetheless, his insides stirred. She had foregone the unsightly bonnet, and her face and golden hair were now visible. Her features, like the rest of her body, were delicate, and her skin was a smooth alabaster. But her crowning feature were her eyes—pale blue and filled with wisdom.

"My dear, why do you stand by the door? Do come in and sit down." Mrs. Briggs pushed herself out of her chair and ushered Miss Greyson into the room. "You've already been introduced to Headmaster Briggs and Mr. Thomas." She gestured toward each of the men. They nodded in greeting before reclaiming their seats. "And may I introduce my daughter, Miss Amelia Farthington."

"Miss Greyson, how wonderful to meet you," Amelia said. "You are exactly as I pictured you to be. Mama was just saying what a marvel you are."

"She exaggerates. I assure you." Miss Greyson's pale cheeks flushed pink.

"Perhaps you are right." A sly smile played on Amelia's lips.

Byron cringed inwardly but Miss Greyson appeared not to

have noticed the slight. She sat stiff and straight on the oversized easy chair across from Byron, her gloved hands clasped together on her lap.

"Oh, my! Amelia said under her breath, just loud enough for Byron to hear. "The girls will have her for breakfast!"

Byron forced a smile.

VIOLET SURVEYED HER surroundings from her plush, armless chair and experienced an odd shrinking sensation. Within the walls of the Ladies' College, she possessed a sense of belonging and usefulness, but that was lost to her in this colorful and lively drawing room. She glanced at the headmistress who relaxed in her chair and chatted amiably with her husband. Suddenly, Mr. Briggs threw back his head and laughed in response to something his wife said.

Violet shifted in her seat, certain there was a rule against mingling with one's teachers outside of school. She hardly recognized Mr. Thomas without his formidable schoolmaster's ensemble. The stiff mortarboard that had crowned his head was gone. And Violet couldn't help but notice that his dark hair fell in thick waves, giving continuity to his long sideburns and complementing his square jaw. Just then, Miss Farthington put a hand on Byron's arm and gave a throaty laugh.

And although he moved his arm away almost immediately—out of respect for the lady's parents, Violet imagined—the brief but intimate gesture left her both uncomfortable and oddly envious. She averted her eyes to her lap.

As though sensing opportunity in her discomfort, Miss Farthington turned her attention from Mr. Thomas to Violet. Tell me, Miss Greyson, where is it you're from?"

"Devonshire." Violet hoped her short answer would detract Miss Farthington from additional prying. She sensed an aura of malice about the woman that cautioned her against revealing too much.

"Really?" Miss Farthington let her eyes wander down the length of Violet's dress.

"Devonshire is a wonderful place. Did you spend much time on the coast?"

Violet smoothed her dress for want of something to do with her hands. "Very little, I'm afraid. I grew up in a small village on the high moors."

Miss Farthington nodded as though Violet's appearance now made sense to her.

"What business does your family do there? Are they farmers?"

"My father is—was—a vicar. But he is no longer with us."

"Oh, I am sorry to hear that. It does explain your somber dress, however."

"Amelia," her mother's low warning drifted across the room and hung in the air.

"I am only taking an interest, Mama. I wish to help Miss Greyson acclimate to her new home." She turned back to Violet. "Is this your first time in London?"

Violet nodded.

"Bright colors are very much in fashion this year. How much longer must you wear mourning clothes?"

"My father died a little over a year ago."

As if they wished to distance themselves from the conversation, Mr. Thomas and Headmaster Briggs rose from their chairs simultaneously and headed for the port.

"Well then, etiquette dictates that you may free yourself of your dark clothing. I have some dresses that I no longer make use of. You must take them and alter them to your liking." She glanced at her mother and smiled.

"That is very kind but quite unnecessary." Violet doubted Miss Farthington's dresses would suit her, and she did not intend to subject herself to Miss Farthington's cruel assessments that would no doubt ensue if she were to accept.

"I understand your reluctance. When my dear Papa died, I thought I would never overcome my grief."

"You were only three years old, dear," Headmistress Briggs said dryly.

"I remember it as keenly as if his death occurred yesterday," Miss Farthington sniffed.

Violet smiled inwardly. She imagined Miss Farthington was the type of woman who'd trained herself to cry and faint on cue. She could not believe such a creature belonged to Headmistress Briggs.

Miss Farthington shook her head, jostling the ringlets that framed her face, as if to toss the sad memories from her mind. Then her countenance brightened again, and she continued her interrogation.

"And what of your mother? Does she live?"

Headmistress Briggs cleared her throat and shifted in her seat, but Amelia paid no heed.

"She died several years ago from consumption." Violet hoped the added detail would satisfy Miss Farthington's curiosity.

"You are an orphan, then. That is sad. Is it not, Mama?" There was no sympathetic tone in her voice, which remained buoyantly cheerful.

"Yes, terribly, but Miss Greyson is a strong and independent woman, nonetheless."

"Do you have any siblings, Miss Greyson?" Miss Farthington asked.

Violet's throat tightened. "None," she managed to squeak.

"You, poor dear! I cannot imagine being all alone in this world. But mother says you are clever, so at least you will be able to provide for yourself. Do you speak French? And play the piano?"

"I do a little of both."

"That is good, Miss Greyson!" Miss Farthington's voice rose as though she were praising a child. "Then you will be sure to find work as a governess once you have completed your courses at the college. Many spinsters do so out of necessity."

"Stop being dramatic, Amelia. Miss Greyson is not alone." Headmistress Briggs's voice teetered on the edge of irritation.

Amelia's lovely eyes grew wide. "Not alone? How wonderful. Then you have a gentleman? Are you engaged to be married?"

Poor Headmistress Briggs, Violet thought. Amelia appeared to be working very hard to aggravate her mother.

"Well, Miss Greyson?" Miss Farthington persisted.

Mr. Thomas cleared his throat in an exaggerated fashion, and Violet looked up to see that he had returned to his seat with a glass of port in his hand. "Miss Farthington, would you play a little something on the piano for us?" he said. "I should like to hear what you learned while in France."

Miss Farthington beamed. "Certainly, I will. My music master, Monsieur L'Strang, was an excellent instructor. I am much improved." She rose from her chair. "You will see that my time there was not wasted."

Relief flooded Violet, and she inadvertently glanced at Mr. Thomas and smiled in gratitude. He caught her gaze and nodded in acknowledgment. Violet immediately diverted her attention to her lap once more. Her heart fluttered. Had she just entered into a secret alliance with Mr. Thomas?

DINNER HAD BEEN a sumptuous meal consisting of soup, fish, tender meats, and fresh vegetables, along with an array of fruits, cakes, and custard for pudding. Still, Byron exhaled with relief when the servants whisked the last of the plates away, and Mrs. Briggs rose from the table, signaling the meal had ended.

Amelia had been insufferable all evening. First, she'd bombarded Miss Greyson with personal questions that were entirely inappropriate. Then, she spent the rest of the evening talking about herself and singing the praises of her piano master,

Monsieur L'Strang.

Had Amelia grown more arrogant during her time in France? Or hadn't he been paying close enough attention before?

"Amelia, you must escort our guest to the library," Mrs. Briggs said. "Miss Greyson is an avid reader, and I am sure she would like to borrow a few books."

"Oh, Mama! What are we to do in the library? I thought to show her some of my dresses."

"I should like to see your library." Miss Greyson's gaze flicked from Amelia to Mrs. Briggs.

"And you shall," Mrs. Briggs said. "There's time enough for both books and dresses. We have a small library at the college, which you may peruse at your will, but our personal library contains many treasures not found there. You may borrow whatever takes your fancy."

"Thank you. That is kind of you."

Amelia sighed with obvious irritation. "Come then, Miss Greyson, and we shall make our way to the library. Will you be joining us, Mama?"

"Thank you, but I think I will leave you young ladies to enjoy each other's company while I attend to a few things."

Byron winced. Had Mrs. Briggs not been present at dinner? Had she not seen the way Amelia harassed Miss Greyson?

The women exited the room, and Collins appeared. "Will you be needing the smoking robes, sir?"

"Oh, yes. Cigar, Thomas?" Mr. Briggs asked.

"Delighted, sir." He accompanied Mr. Briggs to the study. Soon after, Collins reappeared, carrying two smoking robes made from silk, and Byron felt the tension release from his body as he shrugged off his dinner jacket and slipped into the robe.

"So, how do you find Amelia since her return from France?" Mr. Briggs inquired as Collins retreated with the dinner jackets.

"She seems unchanged, I think." Byron kept his voice neutral.

"Unchanged in her affections for you, it seems." Mr. Briggs chuckled. "Mrs. Briggs and I are pleased that Amelia seems willing to attach herself to a sound young man like yourself. She is a headstrong girl, not unlike her mother in that respect, but unlike Mrs. Briggs, Amelia is impetuous. She needs someone who will balance that." He opened his cigar case and offered it to Byron.

Byron extracted a cigar and waited for Mr. Briggs to select one for himself before speaking. "Amelia is only nineteen and likely needs a bit of time to mature."

"I don't believe it's a matter of age but rather a matter of temperament." Mr. Briggs snapped the case shut. "Take Miss Greyson, for example. She isn't much older than Amelia, yet she has a most disciplined and practical way about her, think you not?"

"I imagine Miss Greyson has had a much harder life than Amelia. She is disciplined and practical out of necessity, no doubt."

"I agree, but whatever the reason, you know as well as I do that by nineteen, one's personality is already set. Amelia was educated by the finest tutors, yet she shuns her learning and refuses to use her mind and knowledge for any good purpose. She seems to want a life of complete idleness." He shook his head. "To be honest, I think she has chosen this course as an act of rebellion against her mother. Her father indulged her in her formative years, and she grew spoilt, despite Mrs. Briggs's best efforts."

Byron could not have agreed more, but politeness forced him to stay quiet. He busied himself lighting his cigar, and Mr. Briggs followed suit. Then they both sat down and puffed in silence, taking some time to savor the earthy flavor of the tobacco.

Smoking appeared to have a calming effect on Mr. Briggs. He lay back in his chair, rested his feet on the matching ottoman, and sighed with apparent satisfaction.

"Amelia can be reckless," he continued after a minute's respite. "Her mother and I fear for her future. She is outwardly beautiful and easily flattered by the attentions of men. It would break Mrs. Briggs's heart if Amelia were to be taken advantage of by some young rake. And even if she were to secure a man of title or great wealth, her mother would not want to see her live the life of a socialite."

Byron laughed. "That is the dream of most mothers."

"Yes, but it is not my wife's dream. Mrs. Briggs believes that she was born to change the world, and she will die trying. She has such ardor and passion for her cause, and that is what makes her so dear to me. I cannot allow Amelia to ruin her spirit. Imagine what a failure she will feel if her own daughter chooses to live a life of gossip and idleness. It is the very existence that Mrs. Briggs herself has shunned."

Byron shifted in his seat. "I am a mere schoolmaster; surely Mrs. Briggs has higher hopes for her daughter."

Headmaster Briggs smiled. "Come now, Thomas. You are no mere schoolmaster. You are a Cambridge graduate and an educator at one of the most prestigious schools in England."

Byron nodded. "True, but a schoolmaster all the same."

Mr. Briggs laughed.

Byron eyed him. Had he been too obvious in his exaggeration of this fact?

"Rest assured, Thomas, you will not remain a schoolmaster should you become engaged to Amelia. As you know, I inherited a tidy fortune a few years ago, and I am getting ready to retire. If you are to be my son-in-law, I will not hesitate to recommend you for the position of headmaster."

"But will the governors agree, sir?" Several months earlier, when Mr. Briggs first hinted that Byron could succeed him as headmaster were he to marry Amelia, he'd let the notion float about in his mind as a distant future prospect. And every so often, when the daily minutiae became too tedious to bear and his mood turned black, he'd pluck it from the clouds and make it his savior. Now that the prospect had become a reality, he felt a sense of trepidation. The price was his freedom, and he wanted a guarantee, not a promise.

"The governors will not question my recommendation. They trust me implicitly and have given me the autonomy to run the school as I wish. Nor would I recommend you if I did not think you were fit for the position."

Byron nodded as he digested the headmaster's words. This was the promise he had long been waiting for, yet somehow, he did not feel ready to commit himself to Amelia.

"Mrs. Briggs's hopes that Amelia will mature, as you put it, and start showing an interest in the ladies' college. I doubt that will ever happen, but at least Mrs. Briggs can rest easy knowing that you will be on hand to manage the trust and see to it that the college thrives after she's gone."

"The trust?"

"Mrs. Briggs' first husband was a clever—albeit not a very honest—businessman, and he saw to it that she was well provided for after his death via several investments. The investments grew large over the years, and I sold them at her request. She used the money to fund her school, and she secured the rest in a trust for the college's survival. Those funds are hers to do with as she wishes. We have more than enough with what I have amassed and inherited, but I am afraid that Amelia's future now lies within the walls of that building."

"Does Amelia know this?"

Mr. Briggs nodded.

So, Amelia's chances of marrying into society were even slimmer than he'd realized. No wonder she seemed so eager to be courted by him.

"You will earn a good living as headmaster of St. James's, and I will make sure that you and Amelia want for nothing, but I will not squander my money on her should she make her mother miserable by marrying a fool."

Byron snuffed out his cigar. Things were working out better than he expected. So, why did he feel as though he was about to lose rather than gain something?

Mr. Briggs flashed Byron a conspiratorial smile as though he had his future sealed and locked away. Byron imagined the conversation the headmaster would have with his wife later that evening. *No need to worry, dearest. All is settled.*

Still smiling, the headmaster rose from his chair. "How about I pour us a brandy?"

He placed his cigar in the ashtray and went to pour the drinks.

Byron sat staring at the smoke that spiraled from the burning cigar. Suddenly, the room seemed to be close in on him. Smoke seeped up his nose, crawled in his ears, and snaked down his throat, suffocating him. He felt a strong desire to escape.

"If you will excuse me, sir." He stood and shrugged out of his smoking robe. "I am in need of some fresh air."

Mr. Briggs turned, a glass of brandy in each hand, and blinked. "I've just poured us a drink," he said.

But Byron was already halfway out the door.

CHAPTER SIX

She is not fair to outward view
As many maidens be;
Her loveliness I never knew
Until she smiled on me.
O, then I saw her eye was bright,
A well of love, a spring of light.

—Hartley Coleridge, "She Is Not Fair"

MISS FARTHINGTON'S PRATTLE left Violet wishing she had feigned a headache and gone home directly after dinner. She started to worry that she wouldn't be able to tolerate much more of the woman's company when, thankfully, they entered the library. All at once, Miss Farthington and the noise of her chatter faded into the background of Violet's consciousness.

Illuminated by low gaslight, the library radiated warmth and comfort. A white marble fireplace, sporting an ornately carved mantel, served as its centerpiece. The fire blazing on its hearth enveloped the room in a warm glow and animated a collection of miniature Greek gods that crowded its mantelpiece. Positioned on either side of it, a pair of tall, rosewood bookshelves stood at attention like two wooden soldiers.

"It is mother's favorite room," Miss Farthington interrupted Violet's thoughts, "but I find it rather dull in here."

Violet walked toward one of the bookshelves, brushing past a crimson velvet settee flanked by two matching chairs, which formed a cozy semicircle in front of the flames.

"Do you not enjoy reading, Miss Farthington?" Violet eyed the rows of colorful leather spines.

"That depends on the book." She strolled to the second bookshelf. "Do you like Dickens, Miss Greyson?"

"I read *David Copperfield* and enjoyed it immensely."

"Is that all? Well, then, you must read *A Tale of Two Cities*. It's not his very latest. That's called *Great Expectations*, but he has only released five installments to date. I read *A Tale of Two Cities* at the encouragement of Monsieur L'Strang. We discussed it at length—it's about the French Revolution and the failings of English society."

"Monsieur L'Strang? Your music instructor?"

"Yes, he's a very learned man."

"Did you have music lessons often?"

"Every day, but one cannot always talk about music." A smile played on her lips.

Violet frowned, but she said nothing further on the subject.

Miss Farthington scanned the rows of books. "Monsieur L'Strang enlightened me in many ways," she spoke as though she were hiding a delicious secret. "He encouraged me to read works that would expand my mind." She reached for a book and extracted it from the shelf. "Here is something he gave me that you won't find in Mama's school library."

"Is it in French? It will probably do me good to exercise my French."

"No, this copy is in its original English. The author is British, but his work is more popular in France. She slid the book into Violet's hands and motioned to the settee. "Come, make yourself comfortable, Miss Greyson."

Violet hesitated. Why had Miss Farthington suddenly turned so gracious? Could she have misjudged her?

As though she'd read Violet's mind, Miss Farthington said, "I am sorry that I asked you so many questions earlier. I hope I did not upset you. I can be a little talkative sometimes." She coaxed Violet into a tufted velvet chair.

Violet sank onto the cushioned seat and gazed into the fire, feeling as though she were in heaven. If this were her home, she would spend every waking moment in this room.

"Comfortable?"

"I am, thank you. What are you going to read?"

"Nothing, I'm going to give you some peace. I need to run off and speak to Mama a moment. You can give me your thoughts on the book when I return."

"I would love to."

"I shan't be long," Miss Farthington said, and then she was gone.

Violet inhaled deeply, leaned her head back against the settee, and listened to the soft popping and snapping coming from the fire. How she loved the bliss of silence. She let her eyes roam the room, wanting to take in its full beauty. An intricate beige and gold patterned paper covered the walls, interrupted only by a mullioned window large enough to fill the room with natural light during the day. Heavy crimson drapes, restrained by gold tassels, framed the sides of the window. Violet imagined herself sitting on the cushioned window seat, book in hand, while the sun warmed her body and the trees in the garden sheltered her from the world outside.

Several paintings decorated the walls. One, a depiction of the three muses, hung in a gilded frame above the fireplace. Another sat above a writing desk positioned in the corner opposite the window. It depicted the Amazons in battle. Violet smiled as she imagined Headmistress Briggs sitting tall and Amazon-like at her desk while battling her paperwork.

Violet sighed contentedly and turned to the book on her lap. Its faded-leather cover displayed no title or author.

"Strange," Violet murmured to herself. She opened the book and searched for a title, but the first few pages were completely blank. She flipped the book open and, seeing writing, scanned its contents:

He is now in bed with me the first time, and in broad day; but when thrusting up his own shirt and my shift, he laid his naked glowing body to mine... Oh! Insupportable delight! Oh! Super-human rapture! What pain could stand before a pleasure so transporting? I felt no more the smart of my wounds below; but, curling round him like a tendril of a vine as if I fear'd any part of him should be untouch'd or unpress'd by me, I returned his strenuous embraces and kisses with a fervour and gust only known to true love, and which mere lust could never rise to.

Violet snapped the book shut. For a moment, she sat in stunned silence, her mind and heart racing as she absorbed the shock of the words. Then an angry heat smoldered in her chest. *So, this is the reason for Miss Farthington's sudden turn to graciousness. Is the book her idea of a joke? Does she seek to amuse herself at my expense?*

Violet turned the book over in her hands. Like the front, the back cover lay bare. The only writing appeared on its spine, where the words, *A Book of Manners*, printed in small gold letters, beckoned the innocent reader. Violet grimaced. *A banned book with a false cover! Miss Farthington must have smuggled it into England from France. But surely her music instructor didn't give it to her? Of course not. Miss Farthington is obviously one for deception and lies.* Violet turned to look over her shoulder. She wondered if Miss Farthington had crept back to spy on her from some shadowy corner. Perhaps she was waiting for her to cry out in shock, burst into tears, or faint. Well, she wouldn't give Amelia Farthington the satisfaction of seeing her shocked, or tearful. Violet gritted her teeth and reopened the book, determined to find its true title. Toward the back, sandwiched between several blank pages, she came across a notation scrawled in pencil: *Memoirs of a Woman of Pleasure* by Richard Cleland.

A woman of pleasure? Violet turned the phrase over in her

mind, and the smoldering anger reignited in her chest. So that little minx was trying to make a fool of her. Well, she would not allow that to happen. She may be a vicar's daughter and hail from the uplands of Devonshire, but she was not ignorant. She'd read *Don Juan,* and she would read this book and face Miss Farthington as if nothing were out of the ordinary. Violet turned to the first page and hesitated, but curiosity and pride propelled her forward. At three-and-twenty, she knew little about the relations between men and women—*as any respectable unmarried woman should,* she reminded herself. And yet she wanted to know. Her mind hungered for knowledge about every subject, and although she would not have sought out this information, now that she had it in hand, she could not turn from it. *What if I am to get married one day? I have no mother to educate and prepare me before my wedding night. And I cannot rely on Aunt Prudence for such a thing.* She was all alone in the world, and she hated to feel insensible and vulnerable. Still, guilt nudged at her conscience and urged her to reshelve the book. Then another, more powerful thought came to mind: *What if I never marry? Then I will never know.* And Violet knew that would be the worst of all.

BYRON STARED INTO the darkness. He knew that he should go back inside and rejoin Mr. Briggs, but he could not rid himself of the restlessness that had stirred up inside him again. What was wrong with him? He had accomplished his goal, and it had been easy, so why did he feel dissatisfied? He stood up and paced around the small garden.

It was the idea of marrying Miss Farthington that perturbed him. He had seen her in a new light tonight. Next to Miss Greyson, she seemed unforgivingly vapid. He neither wanted nor needed love—that had brought him nothing but sorrow and pain—but he'd forgotten how much he enjoyed having a like-minded companion to share his life with. Forgotten, that is, until

Miss Greyson had come along and recalled the memory to life.

He reentered the house, but instead of rejoining Mr. Briggs in his study, he headed for the library. He told himself that he needed to check on Amelia—to make sure she wasn't tormenting Miss Greyson again. But, in truth, he suspected that Amelia had long departed the library. It was Miss Greyson, not Amelia, who drew him there.

He trod across the soft carpet that covered the gaslit foyer on the first floor and slowed his pace as he approached the library. The door stood open, and he paused to listen for voices. When he heard none, he edged forward and peeked inside. As he was about to knock, he caught sight of Miss Greyson. She sat on an oversized chair, her back facing him. He entered the room, knowing that he ought to alert her to his presence, but hating to spoil the peacefulness of the moment. He inched closer. Her body was curved forward and her pale neck bent over a book that lay open on her lap.

She shifted in her seat and lifted her head as though she sensed something. The movement jolted him. What if she were to turn and see him standing behind her? He thought about walking back to the door, so he could knock, but that seemed foolish now. Not knowing what else to do, he cleared his throat and said, "I see you have found something to engross you in its pages, Miss Greyson."

"Mr. Thomas!" She leapt from her seat as though he had set it alight. The book slipped from her lap and landed with a thud onto the floor.

"I am sorry to have startled you so." Byron stepped forward and bent to retrieve the book.

"No!" Miss Greyson threw out her hand to stop him.

He paused, momentarily confused, and then picked up the book. He turned it over in his hand and inspected its cover. *A Book of Manners*, he read. Then he flipped it open and scanned a few lines, "*...her lascivious touches had lighted up a new fire that wanton'd through all my veins, but fixed with violence in that center* *appointed by nature where the first strange hands were now busied in feeling...*" He shut the book with a snap and thrust it at Miss Greyson without comment.

She reached for the book. Her hand quivered, and the skin on her neck turned a mottled red, but she managed to snatch it out of his hand. Then she dropped her gaze and fixed her eyes on the book's blank cover.

A heavy silence hung between them, thick, like the air pressure before a rainstorm. Byron ran a hand through his hair. What on earth was she doing with a copy of Cleland's *Fanny Hill?* He'd only glanced at a few lines before recognizing the work. It had been banned soon after its publication in the mid-1700s, but it wasn't uncommon for young men to get hold of an illicit copy and circulate it amongst their friends at boarding school. Mrs. Briggs did not believe in the censorship or banning of books, and her library held a treasury of controversial works. Still, he did not think such a book would be on her shelves, so how did it end up in Miss Greyson's hands? Unless—a thought struck him—he glanced at Violet, and her wide, frightened eyes met his. She threw the book onto the chair as though she were in danger of being bitten by it. "I'm sorry, but I must go now." She glanced at the book again. "I'm truly sorry." She shook her head and scrambled for the door.

Byron moved quickly. "Please," he said, catching her by the arm.

She gasped.

"Wait one moment."

She stilled but kept her gaze directed at the floor. No doubt, she thought he intended to shame her. Byron released his grip on her arm and spoke gently, "Did Miss Farthington give you that book?"

Slowly, she lifted her head and nodded. "She said her music master gave it to her and claimed it would enlighten me."

"Her music master gave it to her?"

"No. I mean, I doubt it."

He nodded. "Of course, she lied to trick you."

"I believe her goal was to embarrass me."

He clenched his jaw. "I am sorry. No doubt, she thought it a good practical joke. Perhaps she has spent too much time in France and forgotten her English manners. I'll talk to her, and she will apologize."

"No! Please. That will only serve to humiliate me, and I will not allow her such satisfaction at my expense."

Byron raised his eyebrows. Amelia was a bully, and not many young ladies would stand up to her. "Good for you," he said, but he doubted that was motivation enough to continue reading a book like this one. There was a reason Cleland's novel made the rounds year after year amongst young men—*knowledge*. Curiosity had compelled Violet to open the book, but interest kept her reading, and judging from how engrossed she'd been in the pages when he'd first entered the library, its contents fascinated her. Violet must have sensed his thoughts because her cheeks reddened, and she averted her gaze. But he was riveted and could not offer her solace by doing the same.

She shifted on her feet, and guilt nudged Byron. He should not have crept up on her and invaded her privacy. He wished he could turn back time, but he could not. There was only one way to make her comfort disappear now and that was to defuse the situation by treating the book like any other. He walked to the chair and picked up the volume. "Tell me, Miss Greyson, what did you make of Cleland's protagonist, Miss Fanny Hill?"

She cocked her head and frowned. "How do know who authored the book?"

Byron shrugged. "It's the type of book young men sometimes get hold of and read."

"You've read it?"

"I have."

She stared at him in stunned silence, and then she began to laugh. "I'm sorry." She slapped a hand over her mouth.

He felt the tension leave the air, and his own body relaxed as a result. "Don't apologize. It's not pure sensationalism. The book has merits beyond its shock value, don't you agree?"

Miss Greyson's blush deepened. "I didn't read enough of it to form an opinion."

Byron understood her hesitation. It was one thing to read such a book in private, and it was quite another to discuss it with a man she hardly knew. But it was too late for polite pretenses, and he didn't want to leave any part of this problem unresolved. If they ignored this, it would sit between them like a sheet of ice and working together would become impossible.

"That is disappointing. I wondered if you thought her a victim of circumstance?"

A flash of surprise crossed her face, and she took a minute to steady herself before replying, "I have some sympathy for the protagonist. She's an innocent young girl, tricked and corrupted by amoral people."

"She is a victim in your eyes, then?"

"Yes."

"I agree that she is victimized initially, but what about later? Is she amoral for enjoying the pleasures of the flesh as much as she does?"

"I read so little—only a few of the first pages—I am not sure what you mean."

Byron eyed her. He knew he should shelve the book and end the conversation, but curiosity propelled him, and he could not make himself stop. "Her first night with the Harlots—she is ordered to lay with one of the more seasoned girls, who gives her a bit of an—education, for lack of a better word."

"I did not read that," she said vehemently, but Byron suspected from the heat that crept across her cheeks that she had.

"Nonetheless," she continued, "it was clear to me that the author was intent on misleading the public."

"How so?"

"By presenting the life of a harlot as pleasurable and fulfilling, rather than what common sense tells one it is—a life filled with desperation, violence, and disease. Of course, I have not read the entire novel, so I cannot comment with confidence, but I have a strong feeling that the author's sole intent was sensationalism and gratification."

"Not entirely." Byron thumbed through the book until he found the passage he was looking for. "As I recall, you are a fan of satire, so tell me what you make of this passage." He cleared his throat and read: *"Imagine to yourself a man rather past threescore, short and ill-made, with a yellow cadaverous hue, great goggling eyes that stared as if he was strangled; and out-mouth from two more properly tusks than teeth, livid lips, and breath like a jake's..."* Byron paused, choosing to skip the next few lines, and then continued, *"This then was the monster to which my conscientious benefactress, who had long been his purveyor in this way, had doomed me."* Byron lifted his eyes from the page to meet Miss Greyson's contemplating stare.

Her face lost its blush of shame and her expression turned contemplative. "Biting satire, to be sure," she said, "but many before have made comments against the lecherous in society without stooping to the low levels of Mr. Cleland."

"For example?"

She paused. "The plays of the Restoration come to mind."

"Most of the Restoration plays are today considered immoral. Have you read any?"

"Very little, I confess. I have read only snippets and several commentaries about them, so I am aware of their reputation, but I am certain, being plays, that they are not quite so graphic. I believe that Cleland's message, whatever it may be, is altogether lost in the depravity of the details."

"There you are, Mr. Thomas!" Amelia sauntered into the room. "Collins said you stepped outside for a breath of air, but you weren't in the garden. Mr. Briggs and Mama will be wondering where you are."

"I was outside, and then I came to the library in search of you, but not finding you here, Miss Greyson and I started a discussion on literature."

"Oh," she said. "Tell me, Miss Greyson, how did you find the book I gave you to peruse?"

Miss Greyson stiffened, and Byron's chest tightened with anger. "What book are you referring to, Amelia?" He turned purposefully and shelved Cleland's novel. "Miss Greyson and I have been discussing the works of Defoe. She tells me that *Robinson Crusoe* was amongst her favorites as a child." He turned and pulled another book from the shelf and handed it to Miss Greyson. "Try this. It too is controversial but far less gratuitous." He glared openly at Amelia, silently daring her to speak.

Amelia shrugged. "I cannot remember what book I gave her," she said with feigned innocence. "One book looks the same as the next to me." She stepped closer to Byron and smiled coyly. "Shall we go back to the drawing room?"

Byron reached for his pocket watch with his free hand and checked the time. "It is almost nine o'clock, and I have a long week ahead of me. So, I will stop in to bid your parents goodnight and then escort Miss Greyson to her carriage."

"As you wish." Amelia pushed out her bottom lip. "Good-night to the both of you, then." She said and sauntered out of the room.

Violet glanced at the book he'd selected for her. "*The Fortunes and Misfortunes of the Famous Moll Flanders*, by Daniel Defoe." She looked up. "How did you know Robinson Crusoe was amongst my favorites as a child?"

"You mentioned it during our interview."

She bit her lip as if to stifle her emerging smile.

He nodded toward the book in her hands. "Have you read *Moll Flanders*?"

"No, I have not had the opportunity."

"Many think it is not fit reading for women."

"Do you believe that?" Her face creased with apparent concern.

"Of course not. But I would be curious to know your opinion

of the book—as a fellow admirer of Defoe, that is."

Her expression relaxed, and she smiled. "Then you shall have it," she said.

CHAPTER SEVEN

Never seek to tell thy love
Love that never told can be
For the gentle wind does move
Silently, invisibly

—William Blake, "Love's Secret"

A SHARP KNOCK delivered to Violet's bedroom door roused her out of her sleep. She'd barely had time to open her eyes before a maidservant, carrying a large, copper water jug and wearing a small towel on her arm, bustled into her room. Violet struggled to a sitting position and clutched her bed covers to her chest, somewhat embarrassed at having a stranger enter her room while she lay in her bedclothes. The maidservant, either unaware of or unconcerned by Violet's unease, marched directly to the washbasin that stood in the corner of the room and emptied the jug of water into it. Then she slung the towel and a washcloth onto the rail attached to the washstand and turned to face Violet.

She was a sturdy woman who looked like she was used to hard work. Her cheeks had a ruddy, slapped appearance, and her hair was a tangle of fiery red curls that refused to be contained under her bonnet. "You had best get to washin' right away, or that water will get cold. Warm water is a luxury that shouldn't be wasted."

Violet nodded. "I know that."

The maidservant continued to observe her as though she were waiting for something. Violet tightened her grip on her covers and made no move to exit the bed. *Why did she not leave?*

"You must be the classics master's new assistant? The one who dined at the headmistress's on Sunday evenin'?"

Violet straightened her body in surprise as though her reflexes had detected some danger. "How do you know that?"

"My sister works over at the Briggs's residence. She told me all about it this mornin' when I stopped by the house to borrow a bit of lard for the cook. The headmistress don't mind that. She encourages it. Anyway, my sister, Sophie—that's her name, she said you must be special because the headmistress isn't in the habit of inviting her assistants to dine at her table."

"Really?" Violet had no idea why the headmistress would single her out for such an honor.

"Yes, an' Sophie sees all the comings and goings in that house." She looked pointedly at Violet.

Violet turned cold as a horrible thought struck her. What if she knew about the book? Could Miss Farthington have boasted to the servants about how she'd played a practical joke on the classics master's new assistant? Violet cringed at the memory of Mr. Thomas's horrified face when he'd unsuspectingly thumbed through the pages of *Fanny Hill*, looking for a title.

"Did your sister say anything else?" she asked tentatively.

"About what?"

Violet shrugged.

The maid placed her hands on her hips. "We don't engage in gossip if that's what you're thinkin'."

"No, of course not. That is not what I meant."

The woman's demeanor relaxed. "Well, I must get on with it—plenty to do. I'm Nellie, and I'll be back to clear away your water in half an hour." She moved toward the door but paused before opening it. "I fetch the laundry on Mondays, so if you have any clothes that need cleaning, leave them out also."

"Thank you, Nellie."

Nellie exited the room, and Violet exhaled her relief. She supposed there would be a lot she'd have to get used to. Even though Headmistress Briggs had given her a room on the top floor, away from the general population of students, living in a building with twenty young ladies along with several maidservants was going to be anything but private.

All she wanted was to crawl back under her bedcovers and hide. How could she face Mr. Thomas without being reminded of that awful book? But that was a luxury she could not afford. She threw off her bedcovers, shivering as her bare feet touched the wooden floor, yet she was determined to be fully dressed and downstairs before Nellie returned to collect the water.

The small fireplace tucked into a corner of the room caught her eye, but this was no time for lighting fires. Mr. Thomas expected her to be at her post at half six, a full thirty minutes before the English lecture started at 7:00 am. This was uncommonly early, she thought, but Headmistress Briggs said that women had to compromise if they wanted a good education. The lecturers were all men who, like Mr. Thomas, had other obligations, so the ladies' college had to operate around their schedules.

It was no matter, Violet thought. She had endured many a harsh winter in her lifetime, and she knew that a little cold wouldn't kill her. Violet tried to bear this in mind as she trembled in her nightdress and worked to secure her hair into a bun. There was no mirror above the washbasin to check her handiwork, but she hardly needed one after years of consistency and practice. Next, she eyed the water. Nellie promised it would be warm, so Violet scooped up a handful and splashed her face. To her great relief, the water was lukewarm, a luxury that allowed her to take extra care while scrubbing herself with the rose-scented soap that Aunt Prudence had given her.

Her father had always been fastidious about personal hygiene, and he had taught Violet to be the same way. The twins had not been as compliant, and she'd fought many a battle with them over the washbasin. After patting herself dry with the small towel, she slipped off her nightgown and hurried into her chemise, drawers, corset, and layered petticoat. She was grateful that she did not own a crinoline, which would have been far too restricting for life in Dartmoor. She hesitated before selecting a skirt from her meager and somber collection, remembering Miss Farthington's comment that bright colors were in fashion. Then she reached for a high-necked black dress—one of several she had sewn in the months after her father's death—and paired it with her Sunday black boots. She wanted to look both respectable and serious on her first day, and she was afraid that she'd given Mr. Thomas the wrong impression during their last meeting.

The memory of it brought a searing heat to her cheeks. She could not understand what had come over her—speaking so boldly about such a vile book. But what else could she have done? He'd caught her red-handed. The thought propelled her to reach for her black bonnet and secure it under her chin. Then she hastened to straighten her bed before slipping out for breakfast.

The residence halls were still quiet, telling Violet that she would be arriving at breakfast earlier than most. No matter. She enjoyed the peace that accompanied early mornings. She made her way down the wooden staircase, the neutrality of which complemented the walls papered in a soft beige, patterned with pale pink flowers. Violet found the color palette soothing and preferred it to the clash of rich colors that decorated the headmistress's home.

She reached the bottom floor and followed the smell of eggs and kippers to the dining hall. The room consisted of approximately eight round tables that accommodated three chairs each. Violet understood from Headmistress Briggs that most of the students were day and evening students, and about twenty young ladies boarded at the school. A long rosewood table at the back of the room housed the food. Two servants worked the table, setting out pots of tea, dishes of scrambled eggs, kippers, bread, and butter. Violet glanced at the large grandfather clock in the corner of the room. The time was 5:50 am, and breakfast did not begin until 6:00. She was grateful to be early. She would take a seat at an empty table and not have to encroach on a group of young ladies who might not want her company.

"Breakfast is not for another ten minutes, miss."

Violet turned to see one of the servants addressing her from the back of the room.

"Yes, I understand," she said. "May I seat myself and wait?"

"Oh yes, come and get yourself a cup of tea first, miss." The round-faced maidservant motioned to her. "Everything is just about ready. I'm going off to fetch some jam for the bread. Then all will be done."

"Thank you." Violet made her way to the buffet table, where she poured herself a steaming cup of tea, added a lump of sugar and some fresh cream.

She placed her cup on a nearby table and enjoyed the silence as she sipped her tea. Before long, she heard the sounds of chatter and laughter in the hallway. Two young ladies aged about seventeen or eighteen entered the room, their arms linked. They were followed by a group of four who talked freely together. They wore satin boots, gloves, and vivid dresses widened in the rear by crinolines. Some wore matching bonnets that were far less conspicuous than Violet's black bonnet, with its large side flaps that swallowed her face, and others went without any bonnet. They wore their hair in low knots that rested on the napes of their necks, with pretty ringlets around their ears.

Upon seeing Violet, the first two young ladies stopped and stared wide-eyed, as if unsure of what to make of her. After a few seconds, they seemed to remember themselves and walked on toward the breakfast table, whispering and giggling together. This pattern of behavior continued as each new group of students entered the dining hall, and Violet began to wish that she had skipped breakfast altogether and stayed in her bedroom.

As the seats in the dining hall filled up, Violet's table remained conspicuously empty. The others avoided her as if she was marked by the pox. Her stomach rumbled as she sipped her last bit of tea, but she hesitated to leave her seat, wishing she had served herself before the other students had arrived. All about the room, young ladies glanced at her before putting their heads close together to whisper amongst themselves. Violet pretended not to notice and gazed into her teacup. It was not as if she had expected to make friends at the school. After all, she was already three-and-twenty, and most of these young ladies were not yet twenty. They would be her pupils, of sort.

"Is this seat available?" Violet looked up to see an exceedingly pretty young lady with a pair of expressive blue eyes looking down at her. "May I sit here?"

"Of course," Violet said.

"Excellent." The girl's pink cheeks dimpled into a smile, but instead of sitting, she placed her books on the seat and scanned the breakfast table. "I'm starving," she said. "I could smell the kippers and eggs in the hallway. I do hope there are some leftovers. It's not every day we have such luxuries, but Headmistress Briggs likes to treat us sometimes. Have you eaten already?" She looked at Violet's empty teacup.

"Not yet."

"Well, do come! Or we will be too late, and I will surely starve to death." She pulled Violet up by the arm. "I am always late for breakfast, and sometimes there is only bread and tea left. And, if I'm lucky, I will still get a scrape of marmalade."

As Violet rose, she became aware of more eyes on her, but her companion did not seem to notice. She linked her arm in Violet's and strode toward the buffet table.

"I'm Miss Hamilton," she said. "And you are Miss Greyson, the new assistant for Mr. Thomas, are you not?"

"Yes, that's correct."

"Headmistress Briggs told me all about you. I assist the mathematics professor, Mr. Raymond, so I'm here to help you 'acclimate'. I think that's how Headmistress Briggs put it."

"You must be very clever. Math isn't my forte," Violet said with an embarrassed laugh, but Miss Hamilton appeared not to care. Her attention had been drawn away by the food.

"We're in luck!" she exclaimed as they reached the table. "There are still some eggs and kippers left. How wonderful!" She piled two scoops of eggs and three kippers onto her plate, followed by a thick slice of bread and jam.

Violet placed a spoonful of eggs and a single kipper onto her plate.

"Is that all?" Miss Hamilton looked at her plate and frowned. "You do know that meals are included in our board and lodging, do you not?"

Violet nodded.

"Do not be shy, then." She heaped another scoop of eggs and two kippers onto Violet's plate. "Headmistress Briggs doesn't believe in the practice of half-starving women for the purpose of appearing ladylike. She says we must eat heartily and need plenty of protein to feed our brains."

"That is too much," Violet protested as Miss Hamilton dropped a thick slice of bread on Violet's plate.

"If you don't eat it, I shall," Miss Hamilton said. "Now, do you want marmalade, butter, or both?"

Violet hesitated. Her stomach was so full of nerves at the prospect of her first day that she doubted she could eat more than two bites. But as Miss Hamilton scooped a spoonful of the bright orange preserves onto her toast, Violet's mind flashed to the little stone kitchen in Dartmoor. She saw her mama, humming to herself as she bent over the range and stirred the contents of a boiling pot, filling the kitchen with warmth and a sweet citrusy scent.

"Marmalade," she said.

"Hold these, and I will fetch our tea." Miss Hamilton shoved her plate of food into Violet's free hand. "How do you take yours?"

"Uhm, cream and one lump of sugar, please."

"I like two." Miss Hamilton smiled and dropped two lumps of sugar into her teacup.

They made their way back to the table, and once again, Violet grew conscious of stares, whispers, and the occasional giggle. Breakfast silenced her companion for a minute as she prioritized getting a few mouthfuls of food down her throat. "Not bad, a bit cold, but that is my own fault," she said after swallowing her third mouthful.

Violet took a bite of bread slathered with a generous amount of marmalade. She savored the sweet and sour citrusy flavor that filled her senses. "That is delicious," she announced upon swallowing.

"Indeed, it is." Miss Hamilton took a sip of tea. "What time are you expected in the classroom?"

The question startled Violet. "Half after six." She turned to look at the grandfather clock in the corner. "I must go now," she said. "It's already five-and-twenty-minutes after six."

"Wait." Miss Hamilton grabbed Violet's arm as she attempted to rise out of her seat.

"What is it?"

"You mustn't think me too forward, but I mean for us to be friends, so may we get the formalities out of the way now?"

"Formalities?"

"I insist that you start calling me 'Ottilie' instead of Miss Hamilton."

"Of course. What a lovely name. Is it French?"

"German. A feminine version of my grandfather's name—Otto."

"That's too beautiful a name not to be used on a daily basis."

"And I may call you Violet?" Ottilie prompted.

"Of course."

"Good, now that's settled, and we are friends, may I make an adjustment to your outfit before you leave?"

"An adjustment?" Violet frowned.

"There is no time to explain now. You shall have to trust

me."

G lancing first at the young ladies around the room and seeing their sly glances in her direction, she nodded her consent.

Ottilie undid Violet's bonnet and slipped it off her head. Then
she loosened Violet's bun and pulled it a little lower, so it rested
on the nape of her neck. She completed her mission by pinching
both of Violet's cheeks.

"Ouch!" Violet said. "What did you do that for?"

"To make your cheeks pink. It's becoming on you." She
glanced over her shoulder and then turned back to Violet. "They
will not whisper and giggle so much now. We'll talk about your
dress later today. Now go on, or you'll be late."

Violet reached for her bonnet, but Miss Hamilton laid her
hand firmly on top of it. "I don't believe you will be needing this
again."

BYRON CHECKED HIS pocket watch and frowned. It was a few
minutes before half after six, and Miss Greyson had not yet
appeared. He'd taken pains to arrive early and thought she would
do the same on her first day, so he was disappointed to find the
lecture hall empty upon his arrival—with the exception of Mrs.
Ward, the class chaperone, who sat snoring in a chair at the back
of the room.

He went to the cupboard and got to work distributing the
inkwells, all the while wondering if his boldness the previous
night in the library had frightened her after all. Perhaps his plan to
normalize Cleland's *Fanny Hill* and treat it as any other novel had
backfired. His behavior had certainly been inappropriate, but he
was only trying to help her save face, and there had been nothing
lewd about their encounter. Yet, the memory of it thrilled him.
He'd hardly been able to sleep because of it.

He consulted his pocket watch again. She was late. His chest tightened. She had every right to feel violated by his conduct—forcing her into a discussion about the notorious *Fanny Hill*. After all, she hadn't chosen the book. And one could not blame her for opening it and investigating its contents. Naturally, she had trusted that any book in her headmistress's house was safe and respectable.

He rubbed the back of his neck, and it felt warm to his touch. What on earth had possessed him to engage in such inappropriate behavior with his assistant? He'd given his word to Headmistress Briggs that he would take care with her education, and he did not imagine that *Fanny Hill* was the type of education she'd meant. He must not, must never, allow their relationship to extend beyond that of master and student again. *Never!*

He glanced at the doorway. Miss Greyson stood in the entrance, her face pink with exertion as though she had been running. "Oh, I see that you are here already. I am not late, am I?"

How long had she been standing there, watching him? Had she seen his distress? His pacing? Had he expressed any of his thoughts out loud?

She smiled at him, apparently waiting for an answer or some response. He realized he had been staring at her and turned away, embarrassed.

"You are late," he snapped. "I had to distribute the ink myself, which is, in fact, your job." He busied himself by extracting his books from his bag and so avoided looking at her, but he imagined the smile fading from her face upon hearing his harsh tone. Guilt nudged at him, but he pushed it aside. It was better to encourage distance. Their relationship needed to remain strictly professional.

"I am terribly sorry, sir. I got turned around. It will not happen again."

"Did the headmistress give you a tour of the building and tell you that you needed to meet your chaperone before I arrived to class?" He spoke without looking at her and busied himself at his podium.

"She did."

"Then you have no excuse." His abruptness met with silence. Despite himself, Byron glanced at her. She remained standing in the doorway, apparently awaiting permission to enter. He straightened, feeling as though he stood on solid ground again. "Come inside, Miss Greyson. Enough time has been wasted this morning."

She entered the lecture hall and walked to his podium.

"Our text is Homer's *Odyssey*," he said. "During our reading, we will explore the ancient Greek culture, the Greek gods and goddesses, and sample the Greek language. Did Headmistress Briggs supply you with the necessary text?"

"Yes." Miss Greyson stepped onto the raised platform of his podium and placed her copy of *The Odyssey* in front of him.

The smell of roses and fresh soap hit his nose, and he stole a furtive glance in her direction. "I believe you, Miss Greyson. I do not need to see evidence of it." He spoke pointedly in the hope that it would cause her to distance herself from him.

But she did not retreat.

"Forgive me, I am uncertain as to my place in the classroom. As your assistant, do I stand beside you at your podium or—"

"No!" He turned sharply, and she stepped back in fright, causing the heel of her boot to catch on the edge of the raised platform. He watched in horror as she lost all balance and flailed toward the ground. He leapt off the podium and broke her fall, catching her around the waist. Her book hit the floor with a soft thump as she lay helpless in his tight grip with the small of her waist cradled in his arm and the heat of her body against his. He looked down at her, and their eyes met. He found himself unable to look away and unwilling to move.

VIOLET HUNG SUSPENDED in the air, Mr. Thomas's strong grip

shielding her against gravity. She held her breath—half terrified and half exhilarated by the close proximity of his body and the sensation of his chest rising and falling mere inches from hers. She felt his gaze travel from her face down the length of her body, setting her nerves alight. As if time had been suspended, he pulled her slowly toward him as he restored her to her feet. She felt the heat of his body and the thrumming of her own heart magnified as the world around them faded.

"Is the young lady unwell?" Mrs. Ward's shrill inquiry snapped Violet back to reality.

The chaperone had evidently chosen that moment to wake up.

Mr. Thomas stepped back abruptly. But Violet, still heady from his touch, swayed unsteadily on her feet.

"Are you injured?" he asked, catching hold of her arm.

"I'm fine, thank you." She steadied herself. "I just feel a bit unnerved, that's all."

"Miss Greyson!" The chaperone's sharp voice sounded again. Violet turned to see the woman fumble with her spectacles.

"I tripped," she said in answer to Mrs. Ward, "but thankfully Mr. Thomas stopped my fall."

Before Mrs. Ward had time to inquire further, the students started filing into the room, and the chaperone sank back into her seat, seeming to accept Violet's explanation.

The students weaved between the aisles filling up the seats, a few turned to glance at Violet and Mr. Thomas as if they sensed something dramatic had occurred in their absence.

Mr. Thomas straightened his posture. "You ought to be more careful," he said in a low voice. "You could have seriously injured yourself." Then he turned abruptly and strode back to his place on the podium with all the stiffness and pomp of a stern master.

Violet remained motionless, uncertain what to do in her role because Mr. Thomas hadn't given her any instructions. Should she take a seat next to the others, or should she stay standing in case Mr. Thomas required her help?

"Miss Greyson." She turned to see Ottilie standing behind her, and relief almost swallowed her whole at the sight of a friendly face.

"I believe this belongs to you." She held out Violet's copy of *The Odyssey,* which was marked "assistant's copy".

"Thank you. I must have dropped it." She felt her face flush.

"Come," Ottilie said. "We had better find a seat. The lecture is about to begin."

Violet glanced back at Mr. Thomas. He stood with his back to the class and scrawled the words *Trojan War* on a blackboard propped up by a large wooden easel.

"I'm not sure what I'm supposed to do. He hasn't given me any instructions."

"Then just take your seat like any other student, and if he wants you to do something for him, like collect papers or help a student, then he will call on you."

Violet let out a breath, relieved to have some direction, and followed Miss Hamilton to locate a seat. All the seats in the front had already filled up, so they had no choice but to sit near the back of the room.

"Who can tell me about the Trojan War as Homer described it in *The Iliad?*" Mr. Thomas's eyes scanned the room.

A young lady sitting in the front row raised her hand.

"Yes," Mr. Thomas said.

"I believe you are mistaken, sir. The text you told us to purchase is titled, *The Odyssey,* by Homer, not *The Iliad.*"

Mr. Thomas's eyes narrowed. "Stand up, please."

The girl hesitated, and Mr. Thomas motioned for her to get up with his hand. "Come, come! I said 'stand'. I want everyone to get a clear view of you."

She rose out of her seat, somewhat hindered by her fashionable hooped dress. But once standing, she turned to glance around the room, her face beaming with pride. Violet recognized her as one of the pretty, sociable girls from the breakfast hall and felt a stab of pity for her. She obviously thought that she was about to receive accolades for her astuteness.

"What is your name?"

"Miss Lawrence, sir."

Mr. Thomas made no acknowledgment of the girl's stated name and instead looked past her to Violet who sat some three rows back.

"Miss Greyson," he said, "Would you be so kind as to stand?"

Violet felt all eyes turn toward her and froze.

"Miss Greyson?" Mr. Thomas repeated.

Ottilie nudged her. "Stand up," she whispered.

Violet stood, wondering if Mr. Thomas meant for her to correct the girl's mistake.

"Miss Greyson, would you please name and describe the two epic poems attributed to the ancient Greek poet Homer?

"The first is *The Iliad*—"

"Speak up Miss Greyson; it is imperative that everyone is able to hear you."

Violet cleared her throat. "The first is *The Iliad,* which tells the story of the Trojan War. And the second is *The Odyssey,* which describes the Greek hero Odysseus's journey home after the war."

"Thank you, Miss Greyson," Mr. Thomas said. "Now, would you please be so kind as to exchange seats with Miss Lawrence?"

Again, Violet hesitated, unsure if she had heard him correctly.

"Make haste, please, Miss Greyson. I have a class to conduct."

A few students snickered and Violet felt a searing heat spread from her neck to her cheeks. She bent to gather her books and cursed her alabaster skin under her breath.

Stealing a quick glance at Ottilie, who shrugged in response, Violet moved down the row of seats toward the center aisle. As she made her way to the front of the classroom, she had the uncomfortable experience of crossing paths with Miss Lawrence, who was making her way to the back of the room. The young woman's round face flushed scarlet with either anger or shame, Violet could not tell which, but she did notice that her eyes glistened with impending tears.

Guilt stabbed Violet's chest, and she opened her mouth to whisper an apology. But Miss Lawrence spoke first.

"Sycophant!" Miss Lawrence hissed in Violet's ear as she passed.

Violet blinked, momentarily stunned by the girl's rudeness. Having lost her siblings years ago, and having since lived an isolated existence, she was not accustomed to petty arguments and insult-swapping with peers. She glanced at Mr. Thomas as she approached her new seat in the front row, but he had already refocused his attention on the class.

"Now," he said, "I will dictate, and you will listen and take down all I say." He paused. "Is that clear?" A rustling of noise filled the room as the students readied their notebooks.

Mr. Thomas put his hands behind his back and paced up and down the front of the classroom. Then he began his dictation. "Homer's Greek hero, Odysseus, begins his homeward journey after a ten-year war with the Trojans." He paused and allowed the students a few seconds to catch up. "The Trojan War, as told by Homer in his epic poem *The Iliad*, started when the Trojan prince, Paris, stole the wife of the Spartan king, Menelaus. Her name was Helen—she is often referred to as 'Helen of Troy'. Odysseus, renowned for his cunning, devised a plan to end the long war."

Mr. Thomas strode between the aisles, stopping to peer over the shoulders of his students in order to check their note-taking abilities. Despite already knowing the information, Violet scribbled to keep up with his dictation. And she felt for some of the others who must have been beyond perplexed by his words. Evidently, Mr. Thomas must have seen as much reflected in their notebooks because he strode to the board and spelled out the words: *Odysseus, Iliad, Spartan, and Menelaus* in large letters. Then he strode toward Violet, holding the piece of chalk in his hands. "Miss Greyson, please write out all pertinent names on the board in their correct spelling as I dictate."

Violet stood, took the chalk, and walked to the blackboard. Mr. Thomas resumed his dictation. As he spoke, Violet carefully spelled out *Agamemnon, Telemachus, Penelope, and Achaean.*

A short trill sounded, indicating the lesson had come to an end, but Mr. Thomas held up his hand to signal the students were to remain seated. "You will forward your notebooks to Miss Greyson before leaving the room. She will make the appropriate corrections to your dictation and return them to you at our next meeting," he announced.

Within minutes, Violet had some forty notebooks piled before her. Tentatively, she opened one. Misspellings and inaccuracies glared back at her, and she shut the offending thing. Worse, Miss Lawrence's insult still smoldered in her chest like a fiery lump of coal. She blamed Mr. Thomas for not introducing her to the class as his new pupil-teacher. Now, all the other students were sure to view her as a toady as well, particularly after they received her corrections to their notes.

"Are you able to manage those?" She looked up to see Mr. Thomas standing over her desk with his book bag in hand, his brow slightly creased and his soft hazel eyes searching her face.

Is that sympathy I detect in his eyes?

Violet swallowed. He thought her incapable. And who could blame him? First, he'd been forced to treat a lurid novel as a work of literature in order to rescue her from Amelia's tomfoolery, and then he'd been called upon again—this time to prevent her from breaking her own neck.

She lifted her chin, determined to demonstrate her confidence and capability. "Of course, sir."

"Excellent. Have them corrected by Monday next." He turned as if to leave and then stopped.

"Miss Greyson," he said.

"Yes, sir." Violet looked up. Hope rose in her chest, but for what, she did not know.

"See to it that you are not late next week." Then he exited the classroom without so much as a glance back in her direction.

She turned to the pile of notebooks, determination replacing her deflated hope. She had exactly one week to prove her worth—both to Mr. Thomas and the students.

CHAPTER EIGHT

The Loadstone Rock was drawing him,
And he had to go toward it.

—Charles Dickens, *A Tale of Two Cities*

FRIDAY ARRIVED AT last, and it seemed to Byron that his pupils at St. James's Academy for Boys had been purposefully obtuse all week. To make matters worse, he was obliged to dine at the Briggs's again on Saturday evening, and he doubted that Miss Greyson would be amongst their guests after the headmistress's disastrous attempt to get her acquainted with Amelia.

When the final school bell sounded at four o'clock, Byron felt an intense urge to escape the building. For what purpose, he did not know. He only understood that he needed to be outside in the open air and embrace his freedom by walking aimlessly, or sitting and doing nothing if he chose.

So, he strolled to St. James's Park and soon found himself crossing its lush grounds without stopping to admire the waterfowl as was his custom. A strong urge to keep moving propelled him forward. Exiting the park on Birdcage Walk, he continued to make his way through the streets of Westminster. And although he had no intention of going to Pimlico, that is where he ended up some twenty minutes later. Once there, he kept his pace until the tall London plane trees surrounding the enclosed grounds of Westminister Ladies' college came into view. Slowing then, he strolled forward with no aim or purpose in mind other than to admire the planes, grown fat with green spring leaves. There was no reason to enter the college grounds at this late hour. He hadn't been scheduled to give an evening lecture, and even those didn't begin until half-after-six, so the young ladies would now be in their rooms reading or studying independently before dinner.

Nonetheless, he walked toward the entrance gate, where he stopped to survey the neatly trimmed grassy area that encompassed the college grounds. Aside from the rustling of the plane trees, stirred by a sudden spring wind, all was quiet. He knew that he should resume his walk before someone spotted him, but he could not pull himself away. So, he stayed motionless, listening to the wind until his agitation passed and a sense of calm came over him.

As he started to turn, he caught sight of a petite figure, clad in black, exiting the building and then strolling across the lawn. Her somber dress gave her away, and he recognized, at once, that it was Miss Greyson. She clasped a book close to her chest as though it were an object precious to her heart and walked with her head down as if deep in thought. When she stopped at the base of a tree, she seated herself on a grassy patch where she opened her book and gave it her full concentration.

Byron continued to watch her. She appeared so engrossed in her reading that she never once looked up from her book—even as two squirrels scampered up and down the tree trunk behind her. He would have been content to remain by the gate and watch her from afar, but the wind had picked up, and he did not want her to look up and notice him. She'd wonder why he didn't come forward and he'd look a fool. So, he pushed the gate open and made his way across the lawn. As he neared her, she glanced up, and the shock of seeing him registered on her face. She started to stand, but he held up his hand to stop her. "Sit, please. I did not mean to disturb you."

Taking no heed of his request, she got to her feet. "Do not concern yourself, Mr. Thomas. You did not disturb me. I was about to go inside. I thought it would be pleasant to sit outdoors in the fresh air, but it's getting rather too windy for my liking."

"Indeed, it is. I had a similar thought when I decided to go for an afternoon stroll. But I noticed you sitting in the garden as I passed by, and I thought I might as well check in with you to see how you are coming along with the students' notebooks." This impromptu lie gave him comfort. After all, it was his duty to monitor his pupil-teacher's progress. He straightened his posture, convincing himself of his authority and right to be there and was somewhat taken aback when her response had a sharpened edge.

"I have been working hard to correct them. There are many mistakes."

"I am sure there are," he said, "which makes proper correction all the more important." But no easier a task to stomach, not that he'd share that complaint with her.

"Of course." She nodded.

Now, he felt somewhat foolish. He hadn't come to admonish her—only to talk.

He glanced at the book she held, but her arm obscured the title. She must have noticed him looking because she held the book out to him and said, "It's *Moll Flanders*. You tasked me with reading it last week."

"Indeed, I did," he agreed. "From the headmistress's personal library."

Her face grew pink, no doubt at the memory of the embarrassment she had suffered that evening.

"What did you make of the infamous Moll Flanders?" He said quickly, wanting to erase that barrier. I am quite curious to know if Mr. Defoe remains an esteemed writer in your eyes."

"Again, Mr. Thomas, you inquire too soon. I am afraid that I have not read enough to form a strong opinion of her character and motives."

Byron's gaze flicked to the book. From the placement of her

gloved hand, he could see that she had read almost half of it. "Come now, Miss Greyson, do not be shy. I only want your opinion. You will not be judged on it."

She swallowed, and Byron could see that she withheld her thoughts. He wondered at this. She had been so open with her opinions on previous occasions. Perhaps he had been too harsh with her during their lessons. The thought upset him. Was her fire so easily extinguished? Her spirit so effortlessly crushed? He hoped not.

"Miss Greyson," he said soberly, "do not make the mistake of containing your thoughts and opinions lest you are challenged or corrected. You will only succeed in impeding your own growth. Forming an opinion but being too afraid to voice it because society expects you to keep your mind idle is what I thought you aimed to avoid by advancing your education."

"It is not society I am afraid of displeasing." She lowered her gaze and her cheeks pinked.

He blinked in surprise, then recovered himself. "I am a teacher, Miss Greyson. It is my job to correct my students so that I might help them do better."

Violet nodded and looked as though she wished to say something more, but then she appeared to stop herself. Byron couldn't allow it. He had to know what she thought; suddenly, it was imperative. He couldn't leave until he knew her opinion.

"Well, Miss Greyson? Are you going to answer my question?"

She took a deep breath before lifting her sky-blue eyes to his. "Thus far, I do not care for her character at all, and I believe Mr. Defoe created her as an example of vanity, immorality, and greed."

"Vanity, immorality, and greed?" *Intriguing.* Byron raised his eyebrows. "But what of her circumstances? Do they not account for her immoral actions?"

"To be sure, she is young and rather naive at the beginning of the novel. But I do not believe her decision to give herself away before marriage had as much to do with her circumstances as it did with her vanity."

"How so?"

"Despite being poor, she was not destitute. She had a good and decent position as a housemaid that provided her with shelter and clothing, yet she allowed herself to be seduced by a man simply because he claimed to love her."

"So, you object to the fact that her naïveté led her to mistake lust for love."

"My objection lies not with her naïveté, but with her vanity. You see, beautiful women possess a false confidence that plain women do not. They do not realize that their beauty alone is not enough to procure true love and that once they are conquered, their beauty loses its value—at least for that particular man—and then they will be discarded. That is exactly what happens to Moll Flanders."

It was an astute opinion, though he wondered how well she knew this to be a fact. "You have a rather cynical view of men."

"It is an accurate one if books are correct. I do not have much personal experience to lean on."

"Of course not," Byron said, as a sense of relief swept over him. He decided to ignore the feeling. "But as for Miss Flanders, she learns her lesson early in life, and the consequences are not terrible. She marries her lover's brother, after all."

"True. However, it is a marriage of convenience. And after her husband's death, she continues to use her beauty to ensnare multiple men and continues to marry them merely for the sake of convenience."

"Is a marriage of convenience so terrible? Is it wrong, in your opinion, to desire security and advancement in society?"

"If that security and advancement come by way of a loveless marriage, then yes. I, for one, would rather remain poor."

He scoffed. "You are an idealist because you can afford to be one."

"Can I? How little you know of me, Mr. Thomas." She turned her face from his.

A familiar bitterness collected in his throat. "Love always ends in tragedy," he said. "The sooner you understand *that*, the better."

"I am no stranger to tragedy, but I refuse to let it color my views on how best to live my life." Her body stiffened.

Byron, realizing he'd struck a blow to her heart, softened his tone. "Forgive me. I did not mean to minimize the tragedy of losing a father, but—"

"The loss of my father is not the only loss I have suffered." The perfect mix of ferocity and sorrow in her voice made him blink in surprise. "And I can assure you—" she paused, as if hesitant to continue—"that I felt the loss of those I loved as deeply as you or anyone…" Her voice cracked, and she stopped speaking mid-sentence as though she could not bear to continue.

He felt her pain as acutely as his own and recognized it to be genuine. The pain that accompanies loss, the very worst kind of pain, had been his constant companion for seven long years. What losses had she suffered? He wondered. Had there been a lover in her past? Had she lived through the same agonizing grief he had? Did she still pine for him the way he pined for his wife and babe? Desperate to assuage her pain and loneliness as well as his own, he forgot all decorum and pulled her toward him. She did not resist. And for a brief, beautiful instant, she rested her fragile body against his chest. But their respite was short-lived. As if protesting their impropriety, the wind picked up and swirled around them, tossing the tree branches and making the leaves tremble and hiss.

Miss Greyson pulled herself from his grip as though Mother Nature had shaken her back to her senses. The instant loss of her warmth stung Byron like a freshly reopened wound.

"I must go," she said.

"Yes," he agreed, wishing she'd stay.

She nodded a quick goodbye and then hurried across the lawn toward the residence building.

Byron watched her go, chilled by an emptiness as icy and

unforgiving as the wind.

WHAT ON EARTH was I thinking? Violet's legs raced to keep up with her heartbeat as she scurried across the lawn. *Throwing myself into Mr. Thomas's arms like that? What must he think of me? I promised Headmistress Briggs that I'd prove my worth as a pupil-teacher. And instead of doing so, I've behaved like a puppy in need of attention.*

She flung open the door of the residence building and hurried up the stairs to her room. Inside, she leaned against her closed door, breathing hard. Shame washed over her as she thought back to the embrace, and she propelled herself toward her writing desk, where a pile of notebooks awaited her.

"You must put this right," she scolded herself. And, determining to show Mr. Thomas her worth, she lit her oil lamp, sat down, and got to work—first, revisiting the notebooks she'd already checked, making sure she'd caught all the mistakes and made detailed notes, and then moving to those still unchecked notebooks.

Hours passed before she looked up from her desk in response to a knock at her door.

Violet frowned. Who could be calling at this late hour, when the gaslight in the hallways had been turned off and the boarders were surely undressed and in their nightgowns?

The knock sounded again, and her heart jumped.

She put down her quill pen and walked hesitantly toward the door.

"Who is it?" She asked, her voice unsteady.

"It's Ottilie. Open the door."

Violet dashed forward and pulled the door open to see Ottilie standing before her, wearing a red coat buttoned over her nightgown. She cradled a small tray in the crook of one arm and carried an oil lamp in her free hand. "I come bearing tea and biscuits." She lifted the oil lamp, illuminating two cups of tea and a plate of biscuits arranged on the tray.

"How kind of you." Violet's throat suddenly ached from thirst. She stepped aside to let her guest enter.

"You missed supper. I was worried." Ottilie surveyed the room, and her gaze fell on the notebooks illuminated by the glow of the oil lamp on Violet's desk. "Did you work through supper?"

"I became too consumed by my corrections and lost count of time." She went to her desk and started gathering up the notebooks. "I am afraid I have but one chair. Allow me a minute to put these aside, so you may sit and put your tray down."

"I wouldn't dream of sitting at your desk and interrupting your corrections of Mr. Thomas's precious notebooks. The bed will do—that is, if you have no objection."

"None at all." Violet stopped tidying.

Ottilie settled the tray in the middle of the bed and seated herself beside it. "Drink your tea before it loses all its heat." She pointed to a floral-patterned teacup. "I added a lump of sugar to yours, but I am afraid I have no cream."

"Oh, never mind the cream." Violet sat down and picked up her cup to take a sip. The sweet, warm liquid filled her with comfort. "This is delicious. It's exactly what I needed." She blinked back unexpected tears as the stress and exhaustion of the past few days caught up with her.

"What is it?" Ottilie reached for Violet's hand.

"Nothing." Violet put down her teacup and shook her head. "It's silly, really. I'm just so grateful for your kindness."

"Then you should know that my motivations are entirely selfish. I consider myself lucky to have you as a friend."

Violet wrapped her hands around the teacup and felt its warmth radiate through her. She'd never known the comfort of a true friend.

"Where on earth did you get tea at this hour?" She asked, after taking another satisfying sip.

"I made it in my room over the fireplace."

"Really?" Violet turned to look at her unused fireplace. "I

didn't realize we were allowed to make tea in our rooms."

"We're not supposed to light fires in the spring. It's a terrible extravagance, and Nellie will be put out because she'll have to clean the grate tomorrow. But I keep a kettle and some tea and biscuits in my room for emergencies, and you missed supper, so what better excuse could I have?" Ottilie shrugged.

"Nellie. Where have I heard that name?"

"The maidservant. You must have met her. She delivers our bathing water in the mornings."

"Yes, of course." Violet nodded. "Well, I am happy I didn't light my fireplace. She seems rather—"

"Intrusive?"

Violet laughed. "A little."

"She's a gossip. She'll ask you million and one questions if you let her. Don't feel obliged to give her any information. Her sister works at the Headmistress's residence, and they like to think they know all the goings-on everywhere."

"She's already told me so—but thank you for the warning." Violet smiled. Then a thought occurred to her. "Do all the boarders have fireplaces?"

"There's one in every room for use in the winter. And I do believe the pupils pay a little extra for that privilege during the winter months."

"But what if they cannot afford it?"

"Most boarders share a room, so the cost isn't too high. Only the assistants and those who can afford to pay extra have their own rooms."

"In that case, I am even more grateful to Headmistress Briggs for giving me this position. In truth, I feel as though I should be paying her for the privilege of being here."

"You are too modest. The headmistress is a sharp business-woman. She treats her pupil-teachers well because we are an investment in her school's future and in the future of women's education—something she cares passionately about.

"As it stands now, Headmistress Briggs must rely on her

husband's connections and influence with the learned men in society to supply her with qualified higher-level teachers. But if she recruits and trains enough young women like us, her school will no longer operate at the mercy of men. It is up to us, and other women like us, to educate future generations of women and help them prepare to do so for others. In fact, Headmistress Briggs says that women must ready themselves and prove that they are as capable as men to study at the likes of Oxford and Cambridge."

Violet's body tingled at the prospect of being involved in such an important enterprise. "Do you truly think it's possible women will be allowed to earn university degrees one day?"

"Not in the near future, no. That is the most radical of ideas. However, if women are not educated at levels beyond basic mathematics and reading, then they will never get that chance. They must take matters into their own hands."

"It seems like a faraway dream." Violet chose a lavender biscuit and nibbled thoughtfully.

"It's a process that will be years in the making, but it will work. Headmistress Briggs, herself, attended Queen's College— the first English institution of higher education for women. And she is not their only graduate who went on to open her own school."

"I did not know women like Headmistress Briggs even existed. I feel as though I have found my true home." She glanced at the pile of notebooks and felt her renewed energy deflate. "There is a lot of work to be done in the area of women's education." Violet sighed. "Our young women have been sorely neglected when it comes to the classics."

"It is no fault of theirs," Ottilie said. "They have been kept from learning because of their sex. But all the women here want to change that."

"You are right." Violet remembered how she would sit outside her father's study with her ear pressed to the door, straining to follow her brother's lessons. Sebastian had hated what he called "the torturous hours" of Latin and Greek and had been only too happy to let Violet complete his homework and transcriptions.

"Are all the students here of their own free will?" Violet asked.

"What do you mean?"

"Take Miss Lawrence, for instance, who called me a 'sycophant' simply because Mr. Thomas made her switch places with me. And the other young ladies—many of them seem rather silly and superficial, whispering and giggling with each other at mealtimes."

Ottilie cocked her head as if trying to better understand. "Bear in mind that, regardless of their wanting to better themselves, they are still young and will act the part. They laughed because your bonnet and dress are…well, antiquated."

Violet's face warmed, and Ottilie reached for her hand. "You do not have to wear expensive dresses to be respected at this school, but if you want to be taken seriously, even at a progressive ladies' college, you must dress for your century. And as for Miss Lawrence, well, she is bitter, that is all."

"Bitter?"

"Her father was recently bankrupted. And with his money went her hopes of marrying an upper-class gentleman. She was not raised by radical thinking parents. And the knowledge that she may one day have to work as a governess and support herself has come as a shock. She has stayed that moment in time by becoming a student, a privilege for which she must depend on her relatives." Ottilie reached for a gingerbread biscuit but paused before taking a bite. "No doubt she has set her matrimonial sights on Mr. Thomas. A teacher at a prestigious public boy's school is better than she might otherwise hope for."

Violet pursed her lips. The notion that any of the young ladies had set their sights on Mr. Thomas annoyed her. "Well, I shall have to grow used to being laughed at because I do not own any fashionable dresses, nor do I have the money to purchase new ones. Furthermore, my father is only twelve months in his grave, so I prefer to wear mourning clothes."

"Granted. Wear your mourning dresses until you feel ready to discard them, but in the meantime, I will teach you how to fix your hair in the current fashion, which will make a considerable difference to how you appear in the eyes of the students."

"But I am perfectly content with my hair as it is," Violet objected.

"Being resistant to change never advanced anyone. Allow me to teach you, and then you can decide how you wish to wear your hair."

"Agreed," Violet said.

"Now, hand me some notebooks and a quill, so I might help relieve you of this arduous task."

"Oh, I couldn't impose on you like that. It is miserable work. The dictations are full of spelling and factual errors. It is as if Mr. Thomas conducted his dictation in Greek instead of English."

"Have you checked mine yet?"

"No, I do not believe so. Shall I do it now?"

"If it pleases you." Ottilie smiled and popped a third biscuit into her mouth.

Violet slid off the bed and searched through the pile of notebooks until she found Ottilie's. She opened it and saw a neatly scripted page, free of inkblots, crossed-out words, or misspellings. She read it with care and found the words to be almost exactly as Mr. Thomas had dictated them. "It is near perfect!" She declared.

Ottilie grinned. "There, you see. Not all the notebooks are terrible."

"You must have had a wonderful governess."

Ottilie shook her head. "No governesses at all, but I did have several tutors."

"Tutors! Your parents must be progressive thinkers."

"Yes, but there's more to it than that, I'm afraid. It's a long story."

Violet positioned her body on the chair to face Ottilie. "I

want to hear if it pleases you to tell me."

Her friend smiled. "My father was a poet, who—"

"Really!" Violet exclaimed.

"Hold our excitement. He was only moderately successful and is now long forgotten. He was also, at least according to my mother—mad."

"I am sorry," Violet said.

Ottilie shrugged. "I do not know it to be a fact, but I do know that he was a heavy drinker and possibly addicted to laudanum, so Mama suffered a great deal during her marriage. He died when I was three, and his final months were particularly hard on my mother. His drinking spiraled out of control, and he squandered most of their money. That is when Mama got it into her head that he was mad. And after his death, she became utterly paranoid that he may have passed his 'madness gene' to me."

"What? Where would she get such a notion?"

"From Ada Lovelace, of course."

"Ada Lovelace? The mathematician? Deceased daughter of Lord Byron?"

"Exactly."

"But what does she have to do with you?"

"After her disastrous marriage to Lord Byron, Lady Byron engaged the best tutors in England to educate Ada because she feared if she allowed her daughter's mind to grow idle, she would—"

"Develop her father's madness," Violet interjected. "I read about that once."

"Precisely."

"And your mother followed suit to prevent the same from happening to you?"

"I believe Mama rather enjoyed the imaginary kinship she created with Lady Byron. She had few others who sympathized with her plight. Society tends to disassociate themselves from those who fall from grace."

"Did you say 'society'?"

"I did, but that world had little to do with our lives. I grew up in Oxfordshire. After my papa abandoned us, my grandfather helped to support us and paid for my education, but he never visited. He remained disappointed in my mama and the choices she made, and since I was the result of her choices, he didn't seem to care to know me."

"And you're his namesake! How sad."

"Not really. When I turned eight, Mama fell in love with one of my tutors—an esteemed mathematician. They married, and I have had a wonderful Papa ever since."

"Your story has a happy ending, then."

"It did. Still, I was lonely at times. I have no siblings, and I had few friends growing up. That's how I developed my love for reading."

"And your mother encouraged you to read novels and poetry? As I understand it, Lady Byron kept her daughter from literature and poetry because she wanted her to have as little in common with her father as possible."

"That's correct. And my mother copied her in that as well. But I naturally pursued my reading in secret. There is nothing so sweet as forbidden fruit."

"How true." Violet nodded, thinking of her embrace with Mr. Thomas in the garden. "How very true, indeed."

CHAPTER NINE

I am undone tonight;
Love, in a subtle dream disguised,
Hath both my heart and me surprised.

—Ben Jonson, "The Dream"

Sleep eluded Byron as the events of the past few days played in his mind. No matter how hard he tried, he could not stop thinking about the feel of Violet's petite body pressed against his chest, or the look of sorrow etched on her face—a sorrow he knew only too well. She'd allowed him to comfort her, if only for a moment, but she too had comforted him and filled his heart in a way it had not been filled in years. The intensity of that moment had been even more powerful than the conversation they'd shared in the library. He felt a kinship with her. She'd suffered loss and lived daily with sorrow, just as he did. And he yearned to know her story.

But it was more than that. Her intelligence, her open honest manner, her astonishing wisdom, and the fiery spirit which lived inside her—in short, all that encompassed her—made him yearn for more.

And that is precisely why he could no longer trust himself. He'd behaved inappropriately in the garden, being too intimate with her, once again. He did not wish to injure her reputation or dishonor her in any way, but once in her presence, something changed inside him. It was as though he lost all control over his own senses. He hadn't experienced such intense emotions since first meeting his beloved Olivia, and he'd sworn never to entertain them again after her death.

Nonetheless, Miss Greyson had come into his life out of nowhere and somehow wormed her way into his hardened heart, and now it was up to him to push her out again. He must resist the pull and set his heart against love once again.

Agitated, Byron threw off his blankets, sat up, and reached for the miniature portrait he kept on the dresser beside his bed. It showed his beautiful Olivia as a fresh-faced young woman, holding their tiny babe in her arms. He'd wanted to prove himself a worthy husband and father more than anything in the world. Too young to protect his mother from the hands of his brutish father, he'd sworn to put things right with his own family. But he'd failed.

No! He would never take such a foolish risk again. Loving another always ended in pain. Seven years had passed since typhus took his family, but the memories were still vivid and the agony endured real. He shuddered. He could not invest himself so completely in another human being again. People were too fragile. Death could take a person at any moment. Losing his mother at the tender age of five had ripped out half his heart, the remainder followed upon the death of his family. He could endure no more. And that is why he felt perfectly comfortable marrying Amelia Farthington. He did not love her, and there was no danger he ever would. A marriage of convenience was far safer.

He reached for the brandy on his nightstand and took a generous gulp. The fiery liquid slid down his throat and warmed his insides. He replaced the decanter and lay back down, but his mind continued to plague him, refusing to let him rest. Brandy had been his helpful sleep-aid and warm companion for the past seven years. But it seemed that tonight, it could not compensate for the delicate curve of a woman's waist. Byron stared at the ceiling and tried to clear his mind, but the image of Miss Greyson continued to creep into his consciousness. She had awakened a longing in him that he had thought dead and buried. *I am undone. Unless I resolve to harden my heart against this woman, I am undone.*

VIOLET SHORTCUT HER breakfast, eating only a boiled egg, which she washed down with a few hurried sips of tea.

"What good will it do you to starve yourself?" Ottilie said as she slathered marmalade onto a thick slice of bread. "How will you think clearly? I should feel half-mad with hunger by tea if a boiled egg was all the sustenance I had to get through the morning's lessons."

"I shan't starve. A boiled egg and tea are more than I can stomach this morning."

"But why are you so anxious? You spent hours correcting those notebooks. Mr. Thomas cannot possibly find fault with them. And it's the first job he's given you!"

Violet patted her mouth with her napkin. She hadn't told Ottilie what had occurred between her and Mr. Thomas in the garden. How could she? How did you explain to someone that you needed to earn back your dignity?

Violet stood up. She was determined to prove her seriousness and her worth, and she planned to have the corrected notebooks in place on Mr. Thomas's podium before he arrived. "I am sure you are right. Still, I must hurry. I don't want to make the mistake of arriving after Mr. Thomas again."

She picked up her carpetbag loaded with notebooks and hurried out of the dining hall. A rush of misty morning air greeted her as she pushed open the door of the residence building and stepped onto the lawn, still wet with dew.

She loved the garden's tranquility at this early hour. It brought back memories of home and gave her a sense of quiet.

Sometimes, she'd close her eyes, inhale deeply, and imagine that she breathed in the fresh Devonshire air again, while her brother and sister chased each other and clamored over the towering tors in the distance. But today, when she closed her eyes, all she could envision was Mr. Thomas embracing her at the edge of the lawn—her body pressed shamefully against his. Only, she hadn't felt shame. She had desired him, and she desired him still.

This truth brought forward a rush of shame and propelled her forward. "Do not think on it!" she muttered and turned her gaze from the offending spot on the lawn. "You are master and pupil—master and pupil," she reiterated as she marched resolutely toward the lecture hall.

The hall stood empty when she arrived, and Violet took the notebooks from her bag to place them in a neat stack on Mr. Thomas's podium. Then she set about distributing the ink and writing quills on each desk. Her nerves formed a knot in her stomach as the minutes ticked by and Mr. Thomas's arrival became imminent. She wanted to make a good impression on him after a bad start last week and yet another embarrassing display of inappropriateness on Friday.

"Miss Greyson."

Violet jerked her head up.

Mr. Thomas stood in the doorway. "I am pleased to see that you have taken pains to ensure your timely arrival this morning, but in the future, you must wait outside until the class chaperone arrives."

It was then that Violet saw Mrs. Ward standing a few feet behind Mr. Thomas. He stepped aside to let her pass, and she tottered into the classroom, leaning heavily on her cane. Violet rushed to offer her assistance. "Shall I escort you to your seat, Madam?"

The woman brushed Violet's arm aside. "Do not fuss, girl. I am not an invalid."

Mr. Thomas strode past her to his podium. Violet held her breath, eager to know his reaction to her carefully marked notebooks, but she kept her eyes on Mrs. Ward, who looked unsteady on her feet. She watched as the chaperone lowered herself into her seat and then shut her eyelids from apparent exhaustion. Violet wondered if Headmistress Briggs had purposefully chosen a partially incapacitated chaperone as a statement of her disdain for the custom.

"What is the meaning of this, Miss Greyson?"

Violet turned. Mr. Thomas stood at his podium and held up one of the composition books. "Why have these been placed on my lectern?"

"They are from last week's lecture." She frowned, confused by the abruptness of his tone. "You asked that I correct them. I assumed you would want to check my notations."

He sighed heavily. "If your corrections require checking, Miss Greyson, then perhaps I should simply correct the work myself— do you not agree?"

Violet swallowed, and to her horror felt the sting of tears prick her eyes. What hold did this man have over her to cause such a flood of changing emotions in her each time they met? He had a maddening way of jumping from sensitivity and kindness one minute to coldness and indifference the next. Her nerves would not bear it if he kept up his erratic behavior. She'd worked diligently on those notebooks, making careful corrections to each and every line in order to prove her commitment and assiduity, and now he would not even give them so much as a glance. Violet pressed her eyes with the back of her hands, determined to put on a brave face. She'd had no idea that being Mr. Thomas's assistant would be so difficult. It was only her second week, and she was already exhausted and mentally drained.

Apparently, Mr. Thomas watched her closely because he scooped up the notebooks and carried them to her. "If you want to be a pupil-teacher, then you must learn to take correction from me without upset and tears."

"I am not upset—only caught off guard that I seem to have done the wrong thing yet again!" Anger and frustration swelled in her chest, but she kept her voice low, not wanting to alert Mrs. Ward by shouting. "How am I ever to do the right thing when you are so changeable? What pleases you one day seems to displease you the next."

Mr. Thomas placed the notebooks on a nearby chair and then turned calmly to face her. "I apologize if I sounded too harsh. I forget you are still learning. And I admit that I can be impatient sometimes. You must not take it to heart."

His apology struck Violet as insincere—patronizing, even. She hated the formal tone he used and the way he stood with his hands behind his back as though he did not trust what they would do if left unrestrained. How could this be the same man who had enveloped her in his arms under the plane tree? She opened her mouth to speak, then thought better of it.

"Speak your mind, Miss Greyson."

"What I have to say is of no consequence." She turned to pick up the notebooks, but he caught her by the arm.

"Come now; I will have nothing less than honesty between us."

Violet glanced at his hand on her arm. Did he mean to rouse Mrs. Ward's attention? She was hard of hearing, to be sure, but she was most certainly not blind. And should she look up—Violet shuddered at the thought. "Very well," she said.

Mr. Thomas dropped her arm.

"It concerns the notebooks. They were a mess—so filled with errors I could scarcely find a correct word on the page. These ladies know nothing about the Greeks or their Trojan war, but that doesn't seem to worry you. You are happy to gloss over it in one lecture and then jump to *The Odyssey*, simply because this is a class for young ladies."

His eyes narrowed. "I think we've already had this discussion, and you know my answer."

But Violet was too angry to stop. She'd spent hours laboring over the notebooks, and he hadn't even so much as glanced at them. She'd been proud of the meticulous notes she'd made to each student, and he'd simply dismissed her efforts.

"For boys, *The Iliad* is paramount—more so than *The Odyssey*. Why should it be different for females? Our goal is to gain equal education to men, is it not?"

"Is it?"

"Yes," she said. "Or perhaps you are of the ludicrous opinion that women shouldn't read certain books lest they damage their thinking."

His body stiffened. "Your point has been made, Miss Greyson. You may return the composition books and then take your seat."

Groups of students filtered into the classroom. He turned and announced, "Cease talking and take your seats. The class will now commence."

The room fell silent with only the sounds of scraping feet and chairs, and the whisper of skirts being shifted and settled.

"Miss Greyson will distribute your ink bottles and composition books. Your task for the next thirty minutes will be to rewrite the dictation incorporating all the corrections she made. She will be on hand to answer any questions you may have until I return." He nodded and strode toward the door.

Return? Was he going to leave her here to monitor these ladies by herself? She was not ready. They would not listen. They would laugh at her. Chaos would ensue.

Panic forced her to speak. "Sir!" she called. Her voice came out in a hoarse squeak. This was a disaster!

He stopped and spun around. "Any pupil who has not completed the corrected dictation upon my return will be dismissed from class for the day," he barked. Then he marched out the door.

Violet turned to Ottilie who looked from the empty doorway to Violet and frowned.

CHAPTER TEN

Since all that I can ever do for thee
Is to do nothing, this my prayer must be:
That thou mayst never guess nor ever see
The all-endured this nothing-done costs me.

—Edward, Earl of Lytton, "The Last Wish"

T HE ROOMFUL OF young ladies looked from their marked composition books to Violet with mutinous glares.

I must not show fear or weakness, Violet thought.

She clapped her hands to get their attention. "You heard Mr. Thomas, ladies. Start making your corrections, and I will circle the room to address your questions." She glanced at Ottilie. "Miss Hamilton, since your dictation was near perfect, you may assist me."

Ottilie gave her a conspiratorial smile and rose out from her seat.

Violet and Ottilie spent the next twenty minutes scurrying up and down the aisles answering endless questions. They had each been summoned by every girl at least eight or nine times. All the students grumbled about Violet's tiny handwriting, which they said was near impossible to read, and protested the pronunciation of Greek words like Achaeans and Andromache.

"Use the hard sound *k* and not the soft sound *ch* for Greek words and names," Violet corrected countless times. Yet the women continued to default to the soft sound.

This and other things kept her so busy that it seemed only minutes had passed when Mr. Thomas walked through the door thirty minutes later, as promised, and strode to his podium carrying several books under his arm.

"I trust that every one of you has completed the corrections to your dictation." He scanned the room.

A collective nodding ensued. Violet wanted to tell him they'd done so without comprehension or any learning that she could see, but she held her tongue and let him take over the class, sure he wouldn't listen to her any way. "Very well. Miss Greyson, Miss Hamilton, you may both be seated."

Violet sat and watched as he opened one of the books he'd brought with him.

"Now," he said. "You have heard how the Trojan prince, Paris, son of Priam and Hecuba, betrayed Menelaus, king of Sparta, who, together with his brother Agamemnon, king of Mycenae, waged war again the Trojans. You have learned that Achilles was the greatest of all the Greek warriors and Odysseus the wisest."

The students nodded in unison.

"Very good. Today, I will read to you Homer's invocation to the muse at the opening of *The Iliad*. It begins in the tenth and final year of the war and details Achilles's wrath at Agamemnon, who has dishonored the god Apollo."

Violet smiled at him. *He had listened to her after all.*

She followed his every movement as he read, with great fervor, the opening pages of *The Iliad*, and wished that he did not have to stop to explain the rudimentary meaning of several words to the other students, many of whom were obviously hearing them for the first time. She longed to listen to him read uninterrupted—this coveted story she'd labored over many times but had only heard read aloud through stolen moments meant for her brother.

BYRON HADN'T FAILED to notice the smile of victory that lit up Miss Greyson's face when he pulled out *The Iliad* and started to read. No doubt, she thought he'd capitulated to her, but she couldn't have been more wrong, and she would find that out soon enough. He still seethed with anger at her earlier impertinence, and he put all of that energy into his reading. The students were transfixed; even Mrs. Ward had put down her novel to listen. But he kept his eyes on Violet in the front row. She appeared to be enraptured by his reading, as though she held onto his every word. Her face glowed and her eyes followed his every movement. She made him feel like a god as he stood on his podium dispensing previously forbidden knowledge as easily as Prometheus had once handed down the secret of fire to man.

When Byron finished reading and put down *The Iliad,* he felt certain that Violet would never question his authority in his classroom again. But he wasn't yet finished. He intended to drive the message home, so it would not be forgotten.

"The Greek goddess of unrestrained pride and insolence is called Hybris, and the Greeks knew all too well the dangers of this common flaw." He looked pointedly at Violet as he spoke. "In the opening passages of *The Iliad,* Homer demonstrates Achilles' wrath and Agamemnon's arrogance, both the consequences of excessive pride. The lack of respect Agamemnon shows Achilles wounds the warrior's pride, so he refuses to participate in the battle against the Trojans. And the Achaeans suffer tragic losses as a result."

He paused to let that fact sink in for the listening women before he continued,

"The hero of the Odyssey, Odysseus, also suffers from excessive pride. As you continue your independent reading of *The Odyssey* this week, you will take note of this flaw in Odysseus and the subsequent consequences. And remember, the ancient Greeks themselves were proud people. Pride is a positive. It only becomes a negative when it goes unchecked."

At that moment the bell sounded, and Byron dismissed the students. He waited for the room to clear and busied himself purposely with his papers and books while Violet collected the inkwells and quills. To his annoyance, Miss Hamilton lingered, no doubt waiting to see if she could be of any assistance to Violet. This irritated him. It was not her job to chaperone Violet. "Is there something you need to discuss with me, Miss Hamilton?" He raised his eyebrows in question.

"No, sir. I only wanted to see if I could be of any help with the cleaning up."

Byron felt his jaw tighten. "Thank you, but this is Miss Greyson's task, and she must learn to manage it by herself. Therefore, you are excused."

He saw Violet glance apologetically at her friend, whose face reddened either from embarrassment or anger.

"Yes, sir," Miss Hamilton said tersely before stalking out of the room.

Violet watched her leave and then turned to give him a look that said, *Was that really necessary?* Of course, she did not articulate as much.

He went back to organizing his papers while Violet worked—cleaning the blackboard, and gathering, wiping, and storing the quills and inkwells. All the while, a stony silence hovered between them.

"May I go now, sir?" Violet asked after she deposited the last inkwell and locked the cupboard.

He deliberately chose not to answer; he was still formulating the right words. Or trying to. She repeated the question, "Will that be all, sir?"

He stared down at her from the platform. "No," he said, and the anger in his voice was palpable. "I have something to say to you."

Violet lifted her chin as though she were a martyr waiting for the inevitable lightning bolt to strike down upon her.

"You are not to question my judgment on what is best for my pupils again, do you understand?"

"I am not sure what you mean," she challenged.

"You know exactly what I mean, Miss Greyson, so do not pretend otherwise. I am talking about your earlier questioning of my judgment to overlook, as you call it, *The Iliad*. As well as your assumptions about my reasonings for doing so."

She raised her eyebrows over flashing blue eyes, and her cheeks reddened. She was very unlike the little woman he'd interviewed. Inexplicably, his heart began to beat faster. She lifted her chin and straightened her shoulders. "I only wished to understand why—"

"Why, you ask? Because these young ladies are *not* their brothers. They do not enter this classroom already schooled in Latin, Greek, and the classics. Therefore, I cannot teach them as I teach their brothers. They have, at best, been taught a smattering of French, math, grammar, and geography along with a great deal of needlework, watercolors, and the serving of tea. *The Odyssey*, in my opinion, is a little more digestible for these young ladies than *The Iliad*."

"You talk of equal education, but you lack faith in your students." Violet's eyes flashed with anger. "At present, society has as little use for ladies educated in the classics as it has for gentlemen proficient in needlework. And that is precisely what needs to change. These ladies have come here expressly for that purpose. And though they are not their brothers, they have something more to offer than your boys at St. James's. They have a desire to learn and a thirst for knowledge."

"Change takes time, Miss Greyson, and you must learn to be patient and to appreciate small steps. You will do well to remember that we are the first, and at present, the *only* ladies' college to offer a course in the classics, which in itself is highly controversial."

Her mouth thinned as she tightened her lips in apparent

disagreement before she continued, "May I ask what made you change your mind, then?"

"Change my mind? About what?"

"You left the classroom and returned with several books, one of which was *The Iliad*, which you then proceeded to teach. It seemed that you went to get it because you agreed with me."

He stared at her. "I did not change my mind about anything. If you must know, I left the classroom because I was feeling vexed and needed a few minutes to calm down. I did indeed go to the library to get a copy of *The Iliad*—but not for myself." He picked up the green leather-bound book and held it out to her. "Take it and translate *The Invocation to the Muse* from English into Greek. We will meet on Saturday in the library at half after twelve to review your work." He handed her a Greek dictionary. "You may use this to aid you. Do you think you can manage that?"

"Of course," she said haughtily.

"Very well. We shall see how you do." He folded his arms.

She gave him a cool stare.

"As for today's lecture," he said, "I confess that it wasn't the one I had planned, but I felt that a discussion on pride was both warranted and necessary. Now, I hope we can agree that the master of this class is the one who holds a tripos in the classics from Cambridge, and not the one who believes she knows better."

Violet opened her mouth to speak, but Byron stopped her. "Do you feel that I have anything to teach you, Miss Greyson?"

She closed her mouth with a snapping sound, then slowly nodded her response.

"And do you wish to learn from me?" He couldn't help to feel satisfied that he'd stopped her from pridefully protesting by reminding her of her place.

Her lips twisted. Clearly, she was holding in what she really wanted to say, but instead—again—she nodded. Her eyes held volumes of hurt and more. Byron forced himself to ignore it.

"Then say nothing further to aggrieve our relationship. Good day, Miss Greyson."

Byron exited the room feeling as if his chest was about to explode. His anger at Violet had been real, but he could not have withstood another moment of the look on her face and the emotions in her eyes, without losing his resolve. Oh, vanity, hubris, and wrath! How well Homer had understood the foibles of man. And what was he, schoolmaster Byron Thomas, but a mere mortal—susceptible to flattery and intoxicated by power.

She made it too easy for him to play God. A single word of encouragement, kindness, or praise would have kept a smile on her face and fueled her passion. Instead, he had crushed her spirit with harsh, admonishing words and cold, disapproving looks. But what choice did he have? He was not a god, after all, only a mere mortal scarred by loss and brought to his knees by grief and loneliness. If he did not subdue her, if he dared to encourage her passionate nature, then desire would consume him, and he would fall from his podium as easily as Troy had fallen after opening its gates to the deceptive "gift" horse.

CHAPTER ELEVEN

But I send you a cream-white rosebud
With a flush on its petal tips;
For the love that is purest and sweetest
Has a kiss of desire on the lips.

—Richard Boyle O'Reilly, "The White Rose"

A CLUSTER OF round rosewood tables populated the common study area of the library at Westminster Ladies' College. Byron's eyes swept the room, skimming over bent heads in search of Violet. He spotted her at the back, quill in hand, hunched over her notebook.

He nodded at the library chaperone, who had been expecting him, and made his way toward Violet. Several students glanced up from their work as he weaved between their tables. They were no doubt wondering what he wanted in their little library. Byron felt their eyes still on him as he approached Violet's table and seated himself across from her. Only then did she look up from her notebook. She didn't smile at him as he'd hoped she would but instead straightened her body and greeted him in a somewhat stilted tone.

"Good afternoon, Mr. Thomas."

"Good afternoon, Miss Greyson. I trust your day has been pleasant thus far." Like her, he kept his tone formal. Not only because they were in a public setting, but because he'd promised himself that there would be no more tomfoolery on his part. He would keep his emotions in check at all times. Their relationship had become too personal, and he resolved to correct that mistake.

"I have indeed. Thank you, sir."

Her body remained stiff, and it wounded him to see her rigid and devoid of that spirit he knew she possessed. But that was the way it needed to be—the way it should have been from the beginning. He knew the change might be difficult for her, but he was unprepared for how difficult it felt for him.

He cleared his throat. "Is the translation complete?"

"Yes, sir." She blew on her notebook to dry the fresh ink and handed it to him.

He glanced at the page and saw right away that she had not translated "The Invocation" from Book I, as requested, but instead translated *Hector's Farewell to his Wife Andromache and their Son* from Book VI. It was a passage that pained him and one he had long avoided.

His first instinct was to reprimand her for her disobedience, but he suppressed his vexation, partly because they were in the library and partly because he wanted to keep things as civil as possible. Instead, he read the passage in silence. The words tore at his heart, but he kept going, making corrections in the margins, not trusting himself to look up or speak to her.

I must go to my wife and infant son, for this may be my last day with them, and it demands a parting word, a tender tear: Today, some god who hates the Trojans, may cause my fall and death by an Achaean hand.

She let him finish without interruption. When he put down his quill and straightened himself to face her, she appeared anxious and blinked at him nervously. She must have seen the irritation on his face. "Is it badly done, sir?"

"No." He folded his hands together and worked hard to keep his vexation from his expression and his voice low. "It is not badly done because it is not done at all."

"What do you mean? I worked diligently on it all morning."

"You know what I mean, Miss Greyson."

"Are you not pleased, then?"

"Pleased?" He struggled to keep his anger in check. "That my pupil cannot follow simple instructions?"

"I am sorry. I should have explained myself before I handed you the notebook. I thought you would be—"

"Miss Greyson, I realize that this is your first experience with any type of formal education, but as you hope one day to be a teacher yourself, you might at least appreciate that students are required to follow the instructions given to them by their masters."

"I understand, sir, believe me. It's only that—"

He held up his hand to indicate that he wanted to hear no more. "I do not need an explanation as to why you blatantly disobeyed my instructions, Miss Greyson. The fact that you feel so willfully entitled to do so tells me all I need to know." He stood. "I am sorry to have wasted your time. I see now that you are more than capable of schooling yourself. Good day."

Aware of his audience, he strode out of the room with as much self-restraint as he could muster.

He kept walking until he exited the building and crossed the front lawn. Only then did he stop and take a moment to regain his composure. He took shelter under the plane trees, pressed his hand to the back of his neck, and breathed evenly. He was unsure how long he stood there before he heard labored breathing and the swish of a dress behind him. Then Violet appeared, panting, by his side.

He glanced at her as she paused to gulp air before speaking. Her complexion was flushed from the chase, and her blue eyes sparkled with energy. She maddened him, yet the urge to take her in his arms and kiss her overwhelmed him. He steeled himself against his desires, determined to maintain his resolve.

"Mr. Thomas, a moment more of your time, please."

"I thought I made myself clear, Miss Greyson."

"You did, sir. And I promise never to be so presumptuous as to disobey your instructions again. But, please, will you at least allow me to explain, just this once?"

"Just this once! You have willfully questioned my judgment from day one. It seems to me that you, a self-schooled country girl, believe you know better than I do. And therefore, you have no need of my assistance. I thought we'd cleared everything up this week, but obviously, I wasted my efforts."

His words must have struck her because she stepped back abruptly. For a moment, he thought she might turn and flee in defeat. But she stood her ground.

"That is untrue. I have the utmost respect for you, and I am grateful for the opportunity to learn from you. You must believe me."

She spoke with sincerity in her voice, but his pride was too wounded to be mollified. "I admit that my hopes for you were high. You seemed an intelligent young lady with a promising future in education, but now I see you are nothing but a willful child, playing at serious learning."

She flinched, and he knew that his words had wounded her deeply. Yet, he did not feel the satisfaction he desired. She stared at him, her eyes revealing her pain. He ached to reach out to her, but he kept his expression firm. She must learn the proper way to do things. He was her master and she, his pupil. Why could she not play her part and keep things as they should be?

Her shoulders slumped in a defeated pose. "I am sorry to have disappointed you. I didn't mean to be willful or to question your authority. I only wanted you to value my opinions. But I see my error now." There was no haughtiness or angry passion in her voice, only acceptance and a lack of challenge. Her spirit was crushed; he'd done that.

He cursed himself. He'd let her down, and he could not bear to see her so discouraged.

She began to walk away. Against his better judgment, he reached forward and caught her by the arm. She stopped but did not turn to look at him. "Of course, I value your opinion, Violet," he said. "Don't you understand that I only wanted you to value mine, too?"

She turned to face him. "I do," she said. "More than you can ever know."

He pulled her towards him, and she folded against his chest. He caught his breath. How was it that she was able to stir his passions so violently? One minute he felt enraged by her, and the next, he wanted nothing more than to hold her in his arms. He knew that he should push her from him, but he could not make himself do it. Instead, he moved both of them farther under the dense cluster of trees so they would be better concealed.

She looked up at him and started to speak, but he placed his finger on her mouth.

"I'm sorry," he whispered, "I tried to be your schoolmaster, but I failed."

"Do not say such things. You have taught me more and better than anyone else."

Her face expressed such intense earnestness that tenderness for her overwhelmed him. He lost all sense of decorum, drew her closer to him, and pressed his lips to hers.

She did not resist.

ALTHOUGH SHE YEARNED for it, Violet had never imagined that she would allow a man to kiss her unless he'd already proposed marriage. But she was unprepared for the sensation of Byron's lips against hers. The kiss heightened her senses and made her tingle with pleasure as though his lips breathed life into her body that had heretofore been asleep.

Decorum dictated that she push him away; after all, how could a man respect a woman who would allow him such free access to her lips? She knew this all too well, yet both her mind and her body betrayed her. And when he slipped his tongue through her parted lips, she met it willingly—even eagerly—and her brain erased all notions of decorum. She gave herself to him, mind and body, with no regard to their positions as pupil and schoolmaster. It felt natural and right.

But when he pulled his lips gently from hers, and the mist of pleasure gradually faded from Violet's eyes, she came speeding back to earth. Suddenly, she stood face to face with her classics master—whom she'd just kissed. His tongue had been in her mouth, and she had enjoyed it. Her breath caught in her throat, and all she could do to hide her shame was avert her face from his. Her legs trembled, and she covered her hand with her mouth in disbelief.

"Violet," Byron whispered and tugged gently at her arm, "look at me."

Her body stiffened. She could not turn to face him. In fact, she might never be able to look him in the eyes again.

"Do not blame yourself." His voice sounded heavy. "It's my fault. I could not restrain myself. I am your schoolmaster, and I should have behaved accordingly." He coaxed her body to turn and lifted her chin with his fingertips to force her to look at him.

"No!" Violet slipped out of his grip. "The fault lies with me. I am the one who should have resisted. My virtue is my responsibility."

"Your virtue is safe, and please know that it will always be safe with me. I will not take such liberties again. I promise to treat you with the utmost civility in the future." His words skewered her heart. How could he turn from passion to civility so easily? She could not endure it. Her nature was too passionate and her feelings too strong. How could she detach herself from him thus?

"It is too late for that," she said. "I am not like you. I cannot switch from hot to cold the way you do. I cannot go from passionate intimacy one minute to dispassionate civility the next, the way you like to. I came here to learn, not to have my heart twisted and pulled in every direction."

"I'm sorry," he said, seemingly taken aback by the accusation.

"Then why do you treat me thus? Do you imagine that I am content to be your plaything?"

"My plaything?" He narrowed his eyes. "Is that where you think my intentions lie?"

She bit her bottom lip, contemplating whether she should proceed and say what plagued her mind.

"Do you accuse me of wanting to turn you into my plaything?" he demanded. "Is that truly what you think of me?" The muscles in his jaw tightened as if he was desperate to keep some damning words from escaping his mouth.

She straightened her shoulders and lifted her chin. "I observed the way you interacted with Miss Farthington at the Briggs's residence. It seems you enjoy a certain intimacy with her. Perhaps there are others, as well."

His eyes hardened and he drew in a breath. "Others? Do you accuse me of being some sort of a—rake?"

"I do not accuse you of anything. I am merely commenting on what I have observed."

He snorted. "Perhaps you have been reading too many romance novels, Miss Greyson."

She ignored this snipe and took a deep breath to help calm her passions before speaking again. "I think that perhaps I gave you the wrong impression of me. I have behaved—" she paused—"I have not been myself lately. I cannot imagine what you must have thought of me after you saw me reading...that book."

"*Memoirs of a Woman of Pleasure?*" He emphasized each word of the title, heightening Violet's agony. "Is that the book you are referring to?"

"You know it is." Violet's voice came out in a shameful whisper.

"So, you have decided that I think you might be someone I can exploit for my own—desires? Entertainment?" He folded his arms. "Well then, perhaps I ought to refrain from teaching young ladies. I would not want you, or any other young lady for that matter, to feel that her virtue might be compromised or exploited by me in any way."

"Do not say such things! I am sorry. I did not mean to call your respectability into question. I spoke out of anger. I am angry at myself because—" She shook her head. "None of the fault lies with you."

"How can that be?" A bitter hurt laced his voice. "Am I not the one who pulled you toward me and forced a kiss upon your lips?"

She shook her head fiercely. "No, that is not how it happened. You know it is not."

"On the contrary, Miss Greyson, I do not know. You accused me of wanting to use you as my plaything, and if I forced myself on you, I must answer for it."

"Stop!"

"Why should I stop? I demand that you make me answer for the offense I caused you."

Her heart raced, and her head spun. She was desperate for him to stop. "You did not cause me offense," she blurted.

He raised his eyebrows at her.

"You did not force yourself on me." She spoke more calmly now. "I willed you to kiss me."

"You *what*?" He moved toward her.

"I yearned for it, and I was glad when you did." Her face heated, and she spun on her heels to run from her shame.

He caught her around the waist. "Why do you run from me, Violet?" he murmured into her hair, using her Christian name again, and the intimacy of it thrilled her. "Amelia Farthington means nothing to me. I have never kissed her as I kissed you, nor do I have any wish to do so."

He turned her body to face his, and Violet trembled with desire as he inched his lips toward hers. But a sound from the street startled them, and they parted abruptly.

"It's not wise to stand here in broad daylight," Byron said.

"The trees don't shield us from every angle."

Violet took a step back. "You're right. We shouldn't be—"

"Will you come with me now?"

"Come with you?" She shook her head, confused.

He reached for her hand. "Please, Violet. Forgive my angry words. You must know that I could never use you as a plaything. You are—you have my utmost affection and respect. I—"

A group of students exited the building and made their way into the garden. Violet glanced fearfully over her shoulder.

"Where will we go?"

He smiled. "That you shall see soon enough."

CHAPTER TWELVE

'Tis time this heart should be unmoved,
Since others it hath ceased to move:
Yet, though I cannot be beloved,
Still let me love!

—Byron, "On This Day I Complete My Thirty-
Sixth Year"

BYRON GLANCED AT the sky. The day's light was still strong, but they needed to make haste, lest it did not last. "Come," he urged, "we must hurry."

"Whatever for?" she asked, as they rushed out of the gates and onto the street. "Can we not slow our pace?"

"No, that will spoil everything."

"I don't understand," she said.

"It's a surprise. I promise it will be worthwhile."

He held out his hand and beckoned her to take it.

She hesitated to retrieve her gloves from her pocket and slip them on.

He smiled and clasped her gloved hand in his.

They hastened up the street, where he flagged down a Hansom cab.

"Why do we need a cab? Are you going to tell me where we are going?"

He heard no fear in her voice, only excitement. She trusted him again, and that warmed his heart. "Not yet. I wish to surprise you."

She rewarded his words with a smile. He ushered her into the cab and gave the driver directions in a low voice before joining her.

The hansom rolled along the streets of Westminster. Violet peered out the window every so often, beaming when she glimpsed the Abbey and Big Ben, but Byron said nothing until the cab turned from Parliament Street onto Whitehall.

"Have you guessed yet?" he asked.

"No. I am embarrassed to say that I am not yet familiar enough with London. He smiled, pleased at the prospect of being able to guide her. She was so wise in some ways and yet so delightfully green in others.

The cab turned onto Pall Mall, and minutes later, rolled to a stop alongside Nelson's Column at Trafalgar Square. Byron grinned at the glee on Violet's face. As soon as her feet touched the ground, she rushed forward and gasped in delight at the dancing fountains, clasping her hands to her chest like a little girl. She spun around, and her eyes climbed the towering commemoration to Nelson. Then she moved closer to inspect one of the four bronze panels at its base.

"It's Nelson's Death at Trafalgar," Byron said, coming up beside her.

She gazed up at the panel and put her hand on her heart. "How poignant and beautiful."

"Yes, it's quite magnificent."

"Is it true they melted enemy guns to obtain the bronze for these?"

"It is, but I would have thought you'd be more impressed that the column is made from Dartmoor granite."

Her eyes widened. "I didn't know that." She smiled at the structure with such tenderness that he may as well have told her that they were made from the stones of her childhood home.

She glanced around the square, which pulsed with life. "Thank you for bringing me here. I have always longed to see it."

"I suspected as much," he said, "but you do realize that I did not bring you here to see the fountains and the statues—delightful though they are."

"I expect you brought me here to visit the National Gallery." Violet turned to face the infamous Neo-classical building that loomed behind the square. "I have read that it has acquired some excellent works since Sir Charles Eastlake was appointed director."

"You know a lot for someone who has never set foot in Trafalgar or the National Gallery."

"You have not set foot in ancient Greece, yet you seem to know quite a bit about it."

He laughed. "Point taken. Now, it is time for you to experience some learning outside of books." He gestured with his hand for her to join him. "Shall we?"

She nodded, and together they strolled around the bustling square toward the gallery.

GILDED-FRAMED PAINTINGS OF all shapes and sizes hung carefully arranged on the maroon walls of London's National Gallery. Violet had never seen anything quite as magnificent or exciting before. She marveled at the building's ornate beauty and the natural light that filtered through its window paneled ceiling. People from all walks of life crowded around the paintings, and Violet was grateful for Byron's guidance and the security of his arm linked firmly in hers. She wanted to stop and inspect every single painting in detail, but he steered her with purpose through the gallery.

"We don't have enough time to study every picture," he told her when she tried to drag him toward a painting that caught her eye. "We must get to the ones I want to show you before we lose daylight."

"But—" Violet began.

"Trust me," Byron said, stepping through an arched doorway into a second gallery room. There he stopped in front of a magnificent oil painting, rich in detail and color. "Come." He positioned Violet in front of him, so she could get a proper look.

Her eyes roamed the width of the painting, devouring its beauty. Never had she seen such a fascinating work of art. The frame, though filled with an eclectic assortment of characters, highlighted only two, and the subject appeared to be their instant attraction for one another. The man leapt from a cheetah-drawn chariot toward the woman, as if compelled to do so. She turned toward him as if caught by surprise. Yet, her face showed no sign of fear. They locked eyes and Violet knew all else faded into the background for the pair. Together, they created a space of their own, but she—the viewer—was invited to share in that intimacy.

"Extraordinary," Violet said, glancing at the label inscribed at the bottom of the painting's frame. "*Bacchus and Ariadne. Titian (Tiziano Vecellio). d. 1522-23. Venetian School,*" she read.

"Are you familiar with the myth of Bacchus and Ariadne—or Dionysus, if you prefer his Greek name?"

"The god of wine and King Minos's daughter," Violet said, still examining the painting.

"He was also the god of fertility and pleasure," Byron said in a low voice.

Violet felt his eyes on the back of her neck, and an exquisite shiver ran down her spine.

She cleared her throat. "I recall the myth about the Athenian hero Theseus, who kills the Minotaur and flees Crete with Minos's daughter." Violet's gaze followed the motion of Ariadne's body in the painting. Titian painted her mid-turn, showing her shift in focus from Theseus, sailing off in the distance, to Bacchus. Her hand still reached out to the ocean, but her eyes were locked on her new lover. "She believed Theseus loved her and would make her his wife. She trusted him enough to spend the night with him on the Island of Naxos. But Theseus's love proved false, and he stole away on his ship while Ariadne slept." Violet shuddered, taking in Ariadne's partially disrobed figure, and imagining her panic and terror upon waking up to find herself discarded. "I recall the shock I felt upon reading this myth. No young girl is ever likely to forget the sting in this tale."

"Its intention, no doubt," Byron said. "But the story doesn't end there. Titian's painting tells a different story. One of a new love." He leaned over Violet's shoulder and pointed to the god of wine, leaping toward Ariadne. "It's as if Bacchus is drawn to her by a force more powerful than himself—a god, though he is. He cannot tear his eyes from her."

Violet felt the warmth of his chest against her back and the heat of his breath against her ear. She turned to meet his gaze. "Nor can she take her eyes off him."

"They've connected—looked into each other's eyes and seen each other's soul," he said.

Violet's breathing shallowed.

A force hit her shoulder, startling her. She broke eye contact with Byron and turned in the direction of the offender. The room came alive again—bright colors swirled before her eyes and a clamor of voices sounded in her ears.

"Excuse me, Miss." A middle-aged gentleman in a brown tweed suit stood before her. "My apologies. Didn't mean to bump you."

She shook her head and smiled, indicating all was well, and the man moved on. Her eyes flicked back to Byron, but the moment was gone. Wanting it back, she reached for it, saying, "Were they happy together? Ariadne and Bacchus?"

"For as long as a mortal and a god can be happy. Their love was true. But Ariadne could not live forever, so once again, love ended with pain."

Byron pointed to a constellation of painted stars that twinkled above Ariadne's head. "He immortalized her, but not in the flesh—she is the constellation, Corona Borealis."

"That is rather romantic."

"It's tragic." Byron scoffed. "Love always ends in loss. No matter if you are a god or a mortal."

She smiled to herself, unwilling to believe his cynicism. He was testing her. "I still think love is worthwhile. You will always have memories of the person you loved after they are gone. And surely the years you spent together are better than being alone."

"Those memories you talk so fondly of will pale in comparison to the crushing pain you will endure when fate wrenches you and your lover apart. Trust me. Love is cruel. It will entice you with its immeasurable pleasure, and then it will bring you immeasurable pain."

Violet frowned. This no longer sounded like a test. "You do not really believe that, do you?"

"Look around you." Byron gestured. "The message is everywhere. Here is another of Titian's masterpieces." He pointed to a painting that hung nearby. "Venus and Adonis. Their story, too, ends in sorrow."

Violet moved eagerly in front of the next painting—too eagerly, she realized, when she saw that it depicted the goddess completely naked and exposed her voluptuous behind as she clutched onto her lover, clad in his hunting dress.

"Adonis wants to go hunting, but she entreats him to stay." Byron moved closer to Violet, and a knot of embarrassment formed in her stomach as they stood inspecting the sensual painting together. "She knows he will be gored to death by a wild boar if he goes hunting, and she cannot bear the thought of losing him. He refuses to listen, and even though she is a goddess, she doesn't have the power to stop Fate."

"How sad," Violet said, forgetting her embarrassment. She swallowed a rising lump in her throat. The poignancy of the painting almost brought tears to her eyes.

"In Shakespeare's poem, Venus is so distraught that she curses all lovers to suffer the same fate—*Sorrow on love hereafter shall attend: It shall be waited on with jealousy. Find sweet beginning, but unsavory end.*"

Violet heard a heaviness come into Byron's voice and glanced fearfully at him.

"So commanded the goddess of love," he said, looking down at her.

CHAPTER THIRTEEN

When to the sessions of sweet silent thought
I summon up remembrance of things past,
I sigh the lack of many a thing I sought,
And with old woes new wail my dear time's waste

—Shakespeare, "Sonnet 30"

A FAMILIAR MELANCHOLY gripped Byron as the old pain that lived inside him resurfaced. It clamped around his heart like Athena's aegis, threatening to turn all thoughts of love to stone. A sudden darkness enveloped him, and he wanted to escape these paintings that depicted love and loss.

"Come," he said, directing Violet's attention to a new painting. "This one's by Damiano Mazza, a student of Titian's." He pointed to a depiction of a massive black eagle gliding past the clouds toward some unknown destination. The beast carried a naked youth on its back and gripped his thigh with one of its sharp talons.

"What's it called?" Violet asked.

"*The Rape of Ganymede.* The eagle is Zeus in one of his famous transformations. He fell in love with the beautiful Trojan boy, Ganymede, abducted him, and carried him to Mount Olympus."

"I don't believe I've heard that myth before."

"I'm surprised," he teased. "And here I thought you were an

expert on *The Iliad*."

Violet laughed. "I don't remember calling myself an 'expert'." She paused. "The myth is referenced in *The Iliad*, you say?"

"Homer tells us that Zeus gave a magnificent race of horses to Tros, the founder of Troy, in exchange for 'the ravish'd Ganymede'."

"The world of the Greeks is a cruel one," Violet said.

"They were showing us the world as it is. The Greeks didn't shy away from human suffering and life's indecencies. Today, we use manners and propriety to quash life's harshness and to disguise our pain, but that doesn't mean it has ceased to exist."

"Did Zeus often transform himself into animals to trick humans?" Violet asked.

"Yes, and not only into an eagle, but all kinds of animals. Here is another of Zeus' conquests that he boasts of in *The Iliad*." He pointed to a small painting, depicting Zeus's abduction of Europa. In the painting, handmaids lifted the young girl onto the back of a regal-looking white bull. The girl's face expressed a mixture of bewilderment and disbelief. Her dress was disrupted, leaving one of her pale, round breasts exposed.

Violet peered at the painting and then took a step back. "The bull looks placid and, well, harmless. Yet, she looks afraid."

"It seems she senses something is amiss. The bull's placidity is a ruse to assuage her fear, so that she will get on his back without a fuss. Once he has her secured, his intentions become clear."

"That's frightening." Violet turned from the painting.

"Do you still think *The Iliad* a good subject for young ladies?" he teased, finding his good humor returning.

"I have read *The Iliad*, yet all of this escaped me, so I don't think it is something you need worry about." Violet smiled, but she no longer felt certain.

Byron looked up at the window-paned ceiling. There was still enough daylight. "I think we have time for one more painting," he said.

"Do they have any by Michelangelo?" Violet asked.

"No originals, but there is a copy of his *Leda and the Swan.*" He escorted her to another part of the room that housed the painting. It depicted a naked Leda cradling Zeus, in the form of a swan, between her legs. The bird's long, white neck snaked up her body and rested its head on one of her breasts.

Byron stood behind Violet and placed his hands on her shoulders as they admired the art together. "It's the Conception of Helen," he said. "The infamous union that led to the destruction of Troy, the deaths of Hector, Achilles, Priam, and thousands of others."

"I never thought about it like that before. It makes it rather dark."

"The aftermath is dark, but the conception is beautiful," he said, looking down at and fighting an internal war to stop himself from kissing the alabaster skin on Violet's neck. She must have sensed his desire because she turned and fixed her eyes on him with such intensity that it made him want to pick her up and sweep her out of the museum. "We should go," he murmured, and she nodded.

His LIPS WERE on hers the moment the carriage door closed. Violet was ready to receive him. Clasping his jaw with her gloved fingers, she opened her mouth and tasted his fresh, clean scent. He gripped her around the waist with one hand and let the other travel from her neck to her chest. His hand grazed her breast, and she gasped from the thrill his touch sent through her body. He pulled his lips tenderly from her mouth and pressed his forehead against hers. "I'm sorry," he said. "I have tried to resist you, Violet, but it seems that I cannot."

His words soothed the aching loneliness that plagued her. "Don't be sorry." Violet arched her body toward his and pressed her lips back onto his mouth. She wanted him to go on kissing her. She wanted to feel the sensation of his hand on her breast again. He must have sensed her desire because he grabbed her bottom lip with his mouth and sucked it as he cupped his hand around her breast. She felt dizzy with pleasure. There wasn't a book on earth that could have prepared her for this moment.

The carriage lurched as one of its wheels rolled over something in the road, and jolted Violet back to reality. She turned her face away from Byron's and fixed her eyes on the window. The world outside blurred as an unbearable shame washed over her for the second time that day. What was wrong with her? She had thrown herself upon him and acted like a wanton woman. Why could she not control herself around this man?

Byron slipped his hand in hers. "I was married once," he said. Violet turned her head slightly to show she was listening.

"We had a little girl."

She heard the pain in his voice and turned to give him her full attention. "What happened?"

"They died within days of each other—first my wife and then our child. It was typhus."

Violet's breath caught in her throat.

"I was glad my wife went first, so she did not have to suffer the loss of our babe. She clung to our daughter until she breathed her last."

"I'm sorry." Violet put her hand on his, understanding his pain and wanting to offer him comfort. Her heart ached, knowing that he'd suffered the same unbearable loss that broke her father and almost destroyed her. His earlier cynicism now made sense. She laced her fingers in Byron's, knowing the only thing that could heal his pain was love.

"That was seven years ago," Byron said, "but I am afraid it plagues me still. The pain comes out of nowhere, triggered by something seemingly innocent." He paused. "I wasn't honest with you this morning. I blamed you for my anger, but it wasn't because you changed the translation passage and disobeyed my orders. Rather, it was the passage you chose to translate that upset me."

"Hector's farewell to Andromache and his son." She gasped, the realization dawning on her.

"Ever since their loss, I have not been able to read that particular section of *The Iliad*. It is, without doubt, one of Homer's most beautiful, but—" He stopped. "You must think me ridiculous."

"What you say makes perfect sense to me." She squeezed Byron's hand. "My mother and younger sister died within days of each other. Consumption took them. I do not know how my father would have borne it without having my brother and me for comfort."

"I thought you had no siblings."

"Not anymore." She swallowed away the lump that rose in her throat. "My brother drowned at sea five years ago." She was surprised at how easily the words slipped from her mouth. Telling Byron felt like a comfort.

Byron returned the squeeze of her hand, encouraging her to go on. "The translation you requested—Homer's invocation to the muse—is one I know well and have translated several times. My brother was a reluctant student and careless with his translations, which distressed my father. He made Sebastian recite the opening to *The Iliad* in Greek over and over again. I would sit on the settee in the study, pretending to do my needlework and mouth the words to him. Last night, when I sat down to translate those same verses again at your request, I found that it recalled a pain so great, I could hardly bear it. So, I chose another. I'm sorry. I didn't mean to cause you pain in return."

"That is what you were trying to explain, but I would not listen." He drew her close to him and wrapped his arm around her. "I am a selfish wretch and would not blame you if you hated me." He kissed her forehead.

"I could never hate you," Violet said, looking up at him. "No matter the circumstances."

He bent down and covered her mouth with his once again.

CHAPTER FOURTEEN

There is a gentle thought that often springs.
to life in me, because it speaks of you.
Its reasoning about love's so sweet and true,
the heart is conquered and accepts these things.

—Dante, "There is a Gentle Thought"

H E ESCORTED HER onto the college grounds, and they lingered for a moment under the shadow of the plane trees.

"Thank you," Byron said.

She tilted her head. "For what?"

"Allowing me to feel joy again." He caressed a loose strand of her hair and tucked it behind her ear.

Violet's pulse raced. She could not believe that after the shame she'd felt in the carriage, she now wanted more than anything to be kissed and touched by him again. He must have felt the same desire within himself because he circled his arms around her waist and pulled her toward him. Violet grew oblivious to their surroundings and to the possibility of being seen.

"I've been lost in a forest of despair for so long." He studied her face as though he could not believe she was real. "And then you arrived, like Dante's Beatrice, to show me the way to heaven."

Violet reached up and touched his cheek. "I, too, have been lost in that dark wood."

He pressed his lips to hers and then opened his eyes and pulled slowly back. "Violet, I—" He stopped abruptly, released his hold on her, and drew back like one awakening from a trance.

"What is it?" Violet asked. "What's the matter?"

"Miss Hamilton," he said. "She's coming this way."

Violet's breath caught in her throat. She turned. Ottilie hurried across the lawn toward them. "Do you think she saw anything?"

"I don't know. I hoped the trees would conceal us, but she might have seen something."

Violet bit her lip, then she forced a smile and waved as her friend approached.

"Here you are!" Ottilie said between breaths. She glanced at Mr. Thomas and greeted him with a curt nod. Then she turned back to Violet. "Where have you been? I've been looking everywhere for you."

"Mr. Thomas took me to the National Gallery as part of my day's lesson. I thought I told you that I had one scheduled today."

"The National Gallery? Just the two of you?" A slight crease formed on Ottilie's forehead.

"Yes, Ottilie." Violet raised her voice slightly. "Along with the rest of the public who were viewing the paintings."

Ottilie lowered her eyes. "I hope you found it useful to your studies."

"I did, indeed. Mr. Thomas taught me a great deal by explaining the mythology behind some of the paintings."

"That's wonderful." Ottilie said, her voice frosty.

"What great urgency made you come looking for me? Has something happened?" Violet attempted to change the subject.

"Nothing terribly urgent. Only that you forgot your notebook and your copy of *The Iliad* in the library. Some of the students said you left there in a great hurry." She paused and glanced at Mr. Thomas. "They seemed to think you were a little upset. I was worried."

Byron's body stiffened, and he clasped his hands behind his back. "I am afraid Miss Greyson left her things behind on my account. The students you spoke to are correct. We had a small disagreement regarding the instructions I gave her."

"The fault was all mine," Violet interrupted. "I have had little experience with formal schooling."

"It's no matter," Byron said. "I left the library, intending to terminate our lesson, but Miss Greyson came after me to apologize. I accepted her apology and decided to change the course of our lesson. Instead of continuing with the translation of Homer, we went to the National Gallery. That is all. I wasn't aware that we had made a scene or alarmed anybody. I am truly sorry if I caused you or anyone else concern."

Byron spoke in a stiff and polite voice with his body angled away from Violet's. She felt as though he'd erected a wall between them, and the chill of it made her heart fold. She took her books from Ottilie. "Everything is fine. You know how people gossip about naught. Thank you for taking care of these for me."

Ottilie smiled and linked her arm in Violet's. "Well, I assume your lesson is over for today. Shall we go inside and get ready for dinner?"

"Yes," Violet said, although every inch of her yearned to stay with Byron. She hated the idea that they should part so uncomfortably after such a wonderful day together. But Ottilie was having none of that. She turned to Byron and said curtly, "Good day, Mr. Thomas."

"Good day, Miss Hamilton," Byron said. "Miss Greyson." He nodded stiffly at Violet.

Violet smiled but could not make any words come out of her mouth. Her heart ached with fear that he was lost to her again.

BYRON CURSED UNDER his breath as he watched the two women

cross the lawn. Miss Hamilton had certainly seen something to arouse her suspicion. It was the only explanation that could account for her overprotective behavior toward Violet and for the disapproving glares she'd fired in his direction. He rubbed the back of his aching neck. What was wrong with him? Had he lost complete control of his emotions? His senses? Was he indeed weak of character—as his father had remarked so many times? He peered at the two figures. They had reached the stairs of the residence hall, and before ascending, Violet turned and looked back at him. He knew, then, that given the chance, he would take the same risk and kiss her again under the plane trees. Such foolishness could only mean one thing—he cared deeply for her.

The thought caught him unawares. He had not expected to develop strong feelings for a woman again. He had set his heart against love many years ago, yet Miss Greyson had managed to crush the aegis that shielded him. How had it happened? That, he did not know. He only knew that the thought of marriage to Amelia now struck him as absurd. How could he have ever considered it? To be chained to a woman who loved no one but herself? That is not what Olivia would have wanted for him. She would not have begrudged him happiness after her death, so why had he punished himself for so long?

He turned and walked toward the gate, thinking of what he should do. He must act with urgency. Tomorrow, he would dine at the Briggs's and put a stop to any notion that he would marry Miss Farthington.

Byron sighed. He wasn't anxious about telling Amelia that he would never marry her because he knew she did not love him. But Amelia liked to be the center of attention, and her vanity demanded that every man fall in love with her. She would be angry for that reason alone. Still, the thought of reneging on his word to Headmaster Briggs filled him with shame. He hoped it would not cost him his position at the school.

There was nothing he could do about it if it did. Life had dealt him too many blows to ignore its blessings. And there was no doubt in his mind that Violet Greyson was a long-awaited blessing.

OTTILIE ALL BUT dragged Violet back inside the residence halls.

"Why do you rush so? Is there a fire?"

"Unfortunately, I think there may be." Ottilie stopped and looked at Violet. Then she threw her arms around her. "Oh, my dear friend! I am so sorry for you. Truly I am."

Violet's nerves sprang to attention. "You're scaring me. What has happened?"

Ottilie bit her lip. "I saw you," she whispered.

"What?" Violet's heart raced.

"Outside. I saw you in the garden with Mr. Thomas."

"I know you did. I was there when you came and returned my books, remember?" Violet laughed, hoping it would hide her guilt. Not only had she turned wanton, but now she'd become a liar as well. *Papa would be ashamed of me.*

Ottilie squeezed Violet's arm. "Stop it, Violet. I saw him—" she paused as two students walked by—"I saw him embrace you, and then I saw him bend forward as though he intended to kiss you," she said in a low voice.

Violet covered her face with her hands. "Oh, I am so ashamed. I cannot imagine what you must think of me."

"I think no ill of you at all. It is him I blame."

"No, you mustn't think poorly of Byron—Mr. Thomas. Please. The truth is," she paused and gathered her courage before saying the words aloud. "I think I have fallen in love with him— and he with me." Violet's ears burned with both excitement and shame.

Ottilie gasped. "Did he declare his love for you?"

"He did not say the words, but—"

"That cad!"

"Ottilie!" Violet protested, and several passersby turned to look at them. "How can you say that?" she hissed, lowering her voice to avoid more stares.

"I must tell you something, or I will no longer be able to call myself your friend." Ottilie looked around the hallway. "But we cannot talk here." She clasped Violet's hand. "Let's go to your room."

Violet's heart banged in her chest as she hurried up the stairs clutching Ottilie's hand. Once inside the safety of her room, she burst out, "What is it? If it is bad news, I cannot bear to wait any longer."

Ottilie slumped on Violet's bed and buried her face in her hands. Violet sat next to her. "Ottilie, please. You really are scaring me."

Ottilie reached to clasp Violet's hand. "I wish I did not have to do this. Promise you will not hate me for it."

"Of course, I will not hate you."

Ottilie took a deep breath and her fingers tightened around Violet's. "You have met Headmistress Briggs's daughter, Amelia Farthington, have you not?"

Violet nodded. She had an inclination as to where this conversation was going.

"I have heard rumors that Mr. Thomas is soon to become engaged to her."

"Rumors?" Violet pulled her hand out of Ottilie's grasp. "So, you do not know if it is a fact."

"No, I have not heard anything about an official announcement, but, well, Nellie and the other maidservants have been talking about it ever since Miss Farthington returned from France."

"The maidservants! Is that all? Didn't you tell me that Nellie gossips and to pay no heed to her?"

"I told you not to answer her questions because she is a gossip. Her sister works at the headmistress's home, remember? The word is that Mr. Thomas has already had a conversation with Headmaster Briggs about asking for Miss Farthington's hand in marriage, and he may do so tomorrow evening."

"Tomorrow?"

"He is to sup there then."

Violet closed her eyes. An image of Miss Farthington's hand on Byron's arm flashed into her mind. She saw them conversing together in the drawing room and heard Amelia's throaty laugh. *No wonder she spoke so rudely to me after finding us alone in the library.* Violet revisited the scene in her mind. Amelia had asked Byron about going for a walk, and he'd declined, stating that it was too late. She pouted when he said that he was going to escort Violet to her carriage instead. She'd seemed rather spoilt and petulant at the time, but now Violet could see the picture from a different angle.

"Even if he has not proposed to Miss Farthington," Ottilie continued, "he seems to have given the impression that he intends to do so. And the way he has conducted himself with you—well."

Violet shivered. It couldn't be true. She remembered his promise to her earlier that day. *"Amelia Farthington means nothing to me. I have never kissed her as I kissed you, nor do I have any desire to do so."* She refused to believe that everything that happened between them was a lie. They'd connected on more than a physical level. She'd felt it. Ottilie simply did not know him as well as she did. She did not understand his pain and vulnerability.

"Violet?" Ottilie interrupted her thoughts.

"I know your intentions are good, Ottilie, and that you wish to protect me because I am your friend. But you are wrong about Mr. Thomas," Violet said, burying the puddle of doubt that pooled in her stomach. "He has revealed his soul to me, and I believe him to be a good and honorable person. He would not hurt me or anyone else on purpose, of that I am certain."

Ottilie bit her lip. "I pray you are correct in your assumptions, but I fear you are naive."

"I am not as naive as you suppose." Violet forced a smile. "So, I will ask you, as my friend, to say nothing more about this." She spoke with conviction, putting another firm layer over the puddle of doubt to stop it from rippling inside her.

CHAPTER FIFTEEN

Out of the day and night a joy has taken flight:
Fresh spring, and summer, and winter hoar
Move my faint heart with grief, but with delight.
No more—O never more!

—Percy Bysshe Shelley, "A Lament"

BYRON STEPPED ONTO the portico of the Briggs's townhome and exhaled deeply before rapping on the door.

It swung open almost immediately, and Collins ushered him inside. Apprehension shadowed the butler's ordinarily stoic face, alerting Byron that something was amiss.

"They are waiting for you in the drawing room, Mr. Thomas." Collins's voice quivered.

"Thank you." Byron stepped inside and then paused. "Are you feeling well this evening? You seem a little out of sorts."

"Not me, sir. I am perfectly well, but I am afraid that—" He hesitated.

Byron frowned. "Go on."

"I am afraid there has been a lot of shouting and angry words in the house tonight, sir." His hands trembled. "I have not been eavesdropping, of course, but they have been so loud; it has been impossible not to hear. All the servants are quite apprehensive."

"Do you mean that Mr. and Mrs. Briggs have been arguing?"

Byron blinked. "That is unusual. I don't believe I have ever seen them quarrel."

"The problem is not between Mr. and Mrs. Briggs. It has something to do with Miss Farthington." Collins swallowed. "And yourself."

Byron felt the color drain from his face. "Something to do with me?"

"I am sorry to say, sir. I hope I am not speaking out of turn, but I wish to warn you so that you are not taken by surprise."

Byron ran his hand over his face. Could Amelia have heard about his and Violet's kiss? If Miss Hamilton had seen them, then others could have spotted them, too. *How could I have been so stupid and careless?*

He straightened himself and patted Collins on the shoulder. "Thank you. Whatever it is, I am sure it is nothing more than a misunderstanding."

The butler nodded, but the look of fear did not leave his eyes.

Contrary to what he'd been told, the house seemed eerily silent as Byron followed the butler to the drawing-room. "You see, I told you there was nothing to worry about. Things seemed to have quieted down already."

Collins nodded but took the unusual step of knocking feebly on the door before opening it. "Mr. Thomas." He announced Byron's arrival and retreated quickly.

Byron felt the tension in the air the minute he stepped into the drawing room. Rather than sitting in their easy chairs, smiling and sipping port, Mr. and Mrs. Briggs stood with rigid poses. Mrs. Briggs faced the window, her back stiff, and she did not turn to greet Byron as he entered the room. Headmaster Briggs acknowledged Byron with a quick nod. He clutched what looked like a glass of brandy—a sign that all was not well. More troubling, however, was the sight of Amelia sitting in a corner chair, hunched over with her head in her hands.

"What happened?" Byron asked.

Mr. Briggs put down his glass of brandy and poured a second

one. He held it out toward Byron. "You had better drink this and sit down."

A whirlpool of panic spun inside Byron. He backed away from the headmaster, declining to take the brandy. "Will somebody please tell me what has happened?"

Amelia stood up and looked at him. Her cheeks were red, and her face tear-stained. "You know full well what has happened," she said. "Exactly what I told you would happen, but you would not listen. You said everything would be fine since we were to be married soon anyway!"

"What on earth are you talking about?" Byron looked around the room in utter confusion.

"Do not feign innocence! Mama and Papa Briggs know everything!"

Mrs. Briggs turned from the window and glared at Byron. "Let's not beat around the bush, Mr. Thomas. Amelia is with child—*your* child."

Byron blinked. He barely had time to digest this information before Amelia rushed to him and threw herself against his chest. "Oh, Byron! Tell them how much we love each other and say we will be married before I change shape. Tell them all will be well."

Byron's knees weakened beneath him. He clutched Amelia by the shoulders and forced her to look at him. "What are you talking about? You cannot be having my child; we have never—"

"Do not deny it!" Amelia's scream cut him off. "Do not pretend! You told me you loved me, and you said that since we were to be married, it would be of no consequence if we lay together."

"What?" Byron said through gritted teeth. He could not believe what he was hearing. He knew Amelia was capable of lies and treachery, but this was too much.

Amelia turned to her parents. "I wanted to wait until we were married." Fresh tears gushed from her eyes. "He said he loved me."

Byron's whole body screamed as if a thousand knives assaulted him. He had never laid a hand on Amelia Farthington, let alone lain with her. This was some ruse of hers. If she was with child, it was most definitely not his child.

"Stop your hysterics and sit down!" Mr. Briggs's voice thundered across the room.

Amelia stopped abruptly and turned to stare at her stepfather. He took a few steps toward her. "I said, 'sit down'!"

Amelia returned to her chair and sat without further argument.

"Thomas." Mr. Briggs gestured with his hand that Byron should sit. Then he handed him the glass of brandy. "Drink it!" he ordered.

Byron accepted the glass and drained it.

"Now," Mr. Briggs said, his gaze shifting between Byron and Amelia, "As you both know, Mrs. Briggs and I are very open-minded individuals—some even call us radicals. We encouraged Amelia to be a free spirit, to read all manner of books, to learn all there is to learn about life—including the pleasures of the flesh. In short, we taught her to enjoy all the freedoms that men enjoy. However, while we might be open-minded, society is not."

"Precisely!" Mrs. Briggs glared at her daughter. "I emboldened you to think for yourself and to take advantage of the freedoms we gave you—the freedom to study, to learn, and to work—not to throw everything away by behaving like a little fool!"

"A fool, am I?" Amelia sprang to her feet. "Do you mean like the great Mary Wollstonecraft you so admire? She bore a child out of wedlock, did she not? As did her daughter, the illustrious author of *Frankenstein*. Correct me if I am wrong, Mama, but did not Mary Godwin become Shelley's lover while he was still wed to one Harriet Westbrook? And let us not forget Miss Evans," Amelia continued, "or should I say, the celebrated George Eliot— a woman you call your friend—who today lives with a married man." Amelia glowered at her mother with a triumphant look on her face, but her tirade wasn't yet over. "These are the women you taught me to admire, Mama. Now you berate me and say I have behaved like a fool. All because the reputation of your precious ladies' college will be tainted. You are not a freethinker after all, are you, Mama? You are nothing but a hypocrite!"

Byron seethed in silence as he listened to Amelia's outburst. She had tried to play the innocent victim. She had attacked his person, accused him of tricking her into laying with him, and of promising her marriage.

As if that were not enough, she now turned to attack her mother. He glanced at Mrs. Briggs. She stared wide-eyed at her daughter, her face etched with guilt and pain. He could see her absorbing all the accusations that Amelia heaped upon her as if just realizing the consequences of her radical talk and thinking. She moved to her chair with the feebleness of one defeated. "You are right, Amelia. I have failed you. Mary Wollstonecraft was so miserable when her lover abandoned her that she attempted to take her own life twice. And poor Harriet Westbrook Shelley drowned herself in the Serpentine… As for Miss Evans, celebrated author she may be, but she and Mr. Lewes are to this day shunned by society. So, you see, my dear, I *have* failed you. I failed to teach you the consequences of being an independent woman and instead allowed you to revel in the glories of it. It should not matter that you conceived out of wedlock, but unfortunately, it does matter. And the consequences will be devastating if you are not married right away."

Mr. Briggs walked over to his wife and placed a hand on her shoulder. Then he fixed his eyes on Byron. "I hope you under-stand the severity of this situation. If Amelia bears a child out of wedlock, all of society will shun her. She will ruin not only her good name but her mother's and mine as well. That will mean the end of Westminster Ladies' College and the end of my career and headmaster of St. James's." He paused. "Your fitness to serve as a teacher—at any establishment—will be questioned."

Byron opened his mouth to protest but stopped himself from speaking. It was clear from Headmaster Briggs's speech that it did not matter whether or not he was the father of Amelia's child.

That point was irrelevant. The only thing that mattered to Mr. Briggs was his wife's happiness. They had fortune enough to survive quite well without their work. Mr. Briggs was nearing his retirement from school life and seemed only to be waiting for Byron to become his son-in-law and relieve him of his duties. But Westminster Ladies' College was a labor of love for Mrs. Briggs. To see it destroyed would all but kill her.

What of my happiness? Byron asked himself. Life as Amelia's husband seemed unbearable now. But Violet would lose her bright future and her happiness if Westminster Ladies' College closed. If she married him, she would be nothing more than the wife of an unemployable schoolmaster who did not have the funds to open his own school. True, perhaps he would be able to find employment in a ragged institution where he would be underpaid, exposed to every type of disease, and stuck teaching basic arithmetic and spelling.

But worst of all, Violet would be forced into a governess position to keep them afloat, the very thing she was trying to avoid with her education. No, he could not endure watching her suffer and seeing her talents wasted. She deserved happiness, and he was no longer in a position to give it to her.

"Well, Thomas, what say you?" Mr. Briggs's words sliced through Byron's thoughts. "Are you willing to do right by Miss Farthington?"

Byron looked up, ready to object to the accusatory words, but the broken look on Mrs. Briggs's face stopped him from speaking. Never before had he seen this strong, vibrant woman look so helpless and defeated. His mind shifted to Violet and the ruined prospects she would face as his wife. Her dreams would end if the college failed and the same defeat that had carved itself into Mrs. Briggs's countenance now clawed at his throat. He had to save Violet's future. He'd not crush his wife's spirit and run her into an early grave like his father had done to his mother. This way, Violet's pain would be short-lived.

Byron met Mr. Briggs's gaze and nodded his consent.

VIOLET SCOOPED UP a spoonful of rhubarb soup and then poured the puree back into the bowl. She sighed as she watched the thin snippets of the vegetable bob on the broth's surface. Then she scooped up another spoonful and repeated the process. Under the table, her leg jiggled up and down as she bounced the heel of her foot on the floor.

The dining hall seemed noisier than usual. She glanced at the smiling faces around the room. Oh, to be happy and worry-free like them. How she wished she could change places with one of these carefree young women.

Beside her, Ottilie scraped her spoon against the bottom of her bowl and brought the last of her soup to her mouth. She swallowed and picked up a thick slice of buttered bread.

"What is the matter, Violet? You have barely touched your food. Do you dislike rhubarb?"

Violet shook her head. "I like it well enough."

"Are you feeling ill, then?"

"Not ill, just not hungry."

"But you must eat something! You barely ate anything at tea this afternoon."

"Really, Ottilie, I am not hungry. It is nothing to worry about. I will make up for it tomorrow." She pushed her bowl toward Ottilie. "You eat it and take my bread, too. Papa taught me never to waste good food."

Ottilie pushed her empty bowl and bread plate aside and replaced them with Violet's full ones. She spooned the soup into her mouth but kept her eyes on Violet.

Violet forced a smile. How could she tell Ottilie the truth after she'd declared her confidence in Byron and made Ottilie promise not to mention him again? But she did not feel confident any longer. Thoughts of Byron dining with Miss Farthington this very night consumed her. And to make matters worse, he'd neglected to contact her all day. She'd hoped he would call on her and waited in anticipation, but her waiting had been in vain. As the time had passed, she'd felt certain that he would send word, explaining his absence, but nothing came—not even a note.

Then doubts started to creep in. She remembered how he'd angled his body away from hers, and now she had no idea how things would be between them when they next saw each other.

She longed to relive the moment she had shared with him in the garden on Saturday. Despite the shame she'd felt for allowing him such free access to her person, she still yearned for him. His touch, his lips on hers, his embrace were all she could think about. But what if Ottilie was right, and his intentions hadn't been genuine after all?

CHAPTER SIXTEEN

When fierce conflicting passions urge
The breast where love is wont to glow,
What mind can stem the stormy surge
Which rolls the tide of human woe?

—*Byron,* "Translation from the Medea of Euripides"

THE ANCHORED SHIP rolled and bounced above the ocean's swell, making Byron's stomach churn. The fiery sun scorched his unprotected skin and burned his salty lips. His legs ached, and he longed to sit down and rest them, but they were lashed at the ankles to the ship's pole, as were his hands. He struggled to free himself. Half-naked men, sinewy and olive-skinned, appeared out of nowhere and wound a third rope around his middle.

"Let me go!" Byron struggled to escape, but they continued to tighten the ropes as if they had not heard a word he had said. "Untie me, you barbarians! Let me go!" He attempted to kick his tormentors but could not move his feet. "Why are you doing this to me?" The men remained deaf to his cries and continued to secure the ropes.

He heard a song in the distance, sung by a voice so beautiful and sweet that it brought tears to his eyes. It beckoned him, and he knew that it was Violet calling to him. He had to break free; he had to get to her. "Violet!" He wrenched against the ropes with all his strength, and they burst open. He ran to the edge of the ship and dove into the clear blue water.

"Come back!" His half-naked captors cried. "You go to your death!"

But nothing could stop him from reaching Violet. He swam toward the angelic voice like a man possessed—and indeed he was—until he reached the rocky shores that held Violet captive. Digging his feet into the sharp rocks, he clawed his way up the steep embankment. With each painful step, the singing grew louder, richer, and more enticing. At the top, he used every ounce of strength remaining to drag himself onto the sand, where he lay blinded by the sharp sun and whispered Violet's name. A blurry form emerged from the woods, and as it came into focus, Byron saw that he'd made a fatal mistake.

Amelia, in the shape of a harpy, strutted toward him, singing her beautiful siren song. She spread her giant wings, ready to ensnare him. He scrambled backward and turned to call for help, reaching for the now distant ship. He could see the men hanging over the side, shouting at him as they retreated deeper into the horizon.

Suddenly, Violet appeared amongst them, like a beacon of light. She waved and called to him. He jumped to his feet and attempted to run toward her, but Amelia's wings clamped around him and smothered him in darkness.

Byron's body jerked, and his eyelids flew open. Dawn's soft rays filtered through the window, and he lay in a pool of sweat amid tangled sheets. Amelia, with her harpy wings, had vanished along with the bright sun and the retreating ship. But the churning in Byron's stomach and the dryness in his parched throat remained. He swung his legs out of bed, sat up, and reached for his bottle of brandy. He swallowed eagerly.

Then he reached for his pocket watch. It was half after five. He flopped back onto his bed and thought about the events that had taken place the night before. What had gone wrong? He had arrived at the Briggs's house resolved to break things off with Amelia and instead he'd given his solemn promise that he would marry her by the month's end! He ran his hands through his hair. But what other choice was there? Mr. Briggs's talk of complete ruin for everyone involved had left him cornered.

And now, he would have to face Violet. How would he explain himself to her? She would think him a liar and a cad no matter what he said.

No, he could not bear to break her heart. It would be better if she came to hate him on her own—if she decided he was not worthy of her. Then she would be the one to discard him. Painful as that would be, he would have to make sure it happened.

"LET ME COME with you," Ottilie urged.

"That is silly. I'll be perfectly fine." Violet forced a light tone. She'd barely been able to swallow her tea, but she had to put on a show of normality for her friend, so she took a bite of toast and pretended to enjoy it. She hadn't slept the night before, unable to stifle thoughts of Byron spending the evening with Amelia Farthington, and now she suffered from a headache.

She just wanted to get to the lecture hall and hear Byron tell her all was well. He loved her and not Miss Farthington. He wanted to marry her and not Amelia Farthington. That is what she needed to hear.

Violet forced a smile, gathered her books, and planted a kiss on Ottilie's cheek. "Do not worry about me," she said and then hurried out of the dining hall without looking back.

Violet slowed her gait as she neared the lecture hall and listened for an indication that Byron was already within its walls. Silence met her ears. Still, her pulse raced as she prepared to enter the room, and she took a deep breath to help calm her nerves. Then she marched forward and entered the room. Her chaperone, Mrs. Ward, sat reading in her chair.

"Good morning, Mrs. Ward." Violet raised her voice to ensure her chaperone would hear her.

Mrs. Ward glanced up and nodded her response. Violet busied herself by cleaning the chalkboard, distributing the ink, and pretending to tidy things that did not need any tidying. Her anxiety deepened as the minutes ticked by, and Byron failed to arrive. If he had met with some accident or fallen ill, Headmistress Briggs would have informed her and canceled the lecture.

What then was the reason for his avoidance of her? She waited in vain, glancing at the clock every few seconds, no longer bothering to keep up the appearance of being busy. The students started arriving a few minutes before seven. Several students glanced at the empty podium with questioning expressions.

Ottilie arrived with the others and rushed to Violet's side. "Is he not here today?"

Violet shrugged, afraid that if she tried to speak, she'd burst into tears.

Byron strode through the door at four minutes after 7 o'clock and went directly to his podium, giving Violet a cursory glance as he did.

"Take a seat, Miss Greyson. The lesson is about to commence."

Violet took her seat and told herself not to overreact. His demeanor was distant and formal, but that was not unusual. Of course, he could not behave the same way toward her in public as he did in private. He had to treat her like any other student. Still, an uneasiness settled in her chest. Something was amiss. He had missed their morning meeting, and she knew without a doubt that he had done so on purpose.

"Miss Greyson, would you be so kind as to join the rest of us in our reading of *The Odyssey?*"

Violet's mind snapped back to the present, and she looked up. Byron averted his gaze and said, "Your book, Miss Greyson, please open it so that we may begin."

Violet reached into her bag, withdrew *The Odyssey,* and opened it.

"Miss Wilson," Byron said, "stand and read Homer's opening from Book V."

As the girl read, he interjected with corrections to her pronunciation. Violet watched his every movement. But if he felt her gaze on him, he did not show it. It was as if she no longer existed to him. Was this the same man who had told her of his personal agony and comforted her when she had revealed her past to him? Was this the man who had caressed her hair and spoken to her in soft, loving tones? Kissed her? Touched her breasts? Her stomach clenched at the last thought.

"Thank you, Miss Wilson. You may sit."

"Miss Cooper, please stand and continue with the reading."

Violet tried to catch his eye, but he avoided her gaze. She remembered how he had wrapped his arms around her waist and pulled her close to him as if he could not bear any distance between them. What had happened? It seemed that all he wanted now was distance. She gazed at his mouth and imagined the softness of his lips against hers. He must have felt the intensity of her stare because he glanced at her, and in that tiny instant, she could see the old desire on his face. But with one blink, it disappeared.

"That is enough, Miss Cooper. No! Do not sit. Did I ask you to be seated?"

"No, sir."

"Quite right. Remain standing and explain to us what you have just read."

Miss Cooper remained silent.

"Well?" Byron said.

"I am sorry, Mr. Thomas, but despite being able to read the words, I am unable to make sense of them in my mind."

Byron sighed. "Would anyone else like to attempt to explain the passage?"

Violet raised her hand. Byron appeared to deliberately ignore her, scanning the class for another student to choose.

"Yes, Miss Evans? Please stand."

Violet's lip trembled as she listened to Miss Evans fumble through an explanation of the passage. He had deliberately slighted her. He had held her, comforted her, and kissed her, and now he wished to scorn her. Perhaps Ottilie had been correct, and he was, in fact, a cad who was already engaged to Miss Farthington?

An involuntary tear slid down her cheek. She withdrew a handkerchief and blew her nose attempting to hide her agony.

"Thank you, Miss Evans. You may sit. Notebooks out for dictation."

There was a bustle of noise as the students retrieved their notebooks.

"Miss Hamilton, would you be so kind as to distribute the ink?"

"It is already done, sir," Ottilie said.

Byron frowned and nodded. "Let us begin, then. Odysseus had been away from Ithaca for ten long years and is anxious to return to his faithful wife Penelope and their son Telemachus."

The scratch of quills on paper sounded all around, and Byron began his march up and down the aisles as he dictated, but Violet could not bring herself to write. She stared ahead as her confusion and humiliation turning to anger.

Byron stopped beside her desk. She felt his eyes on her empty notebook but refused to look at him. He stepped forward as if to continue his march, then he paused and turned back, coming to lean over her desk.

She inhaled his scent and, finding herself close to tears again, held her breath, willing him to go.

"Are you unwell?" he asked in a low voice.

She nodded. An angry tear slipped down her cheek.

"Then you may be excused." His tone was gentle, which made Violet's face burn with shame. She snatched her belongings and rushed out of the classroom. As she exited, she heard Byron order, "Miss Greyson has been excused, but you have not, Miss Hamilton."

BYRON TURNED HIS back to the class, so they could not see his anguish. Treating Violet with such coldness was unbearable. The thought of her suffering on his account moved like a hot knife in his gut. But what choice did he have? The sooner he made her hate him, the better for her. Painful though it was, he had to accept that Violet was lost to him. He was to be Amelia Farthington's husband by the month's end, and he needed to make Violet regret their attachment before that happened.

A low murmur sounded behind him, and he realized the students were becoming restless. He squared his shoulders and turned to face the class. "Right, let us continue—" He pressed his fingers to his forehead, desperate to clear his mind so he could think straight. But all he could do was think of Violet. *How confused, hurt, and alone she must feel. Why had he prevented Miss Hamilton from accompanying her?*

One young lady coughed politely, and Byron looked up to see his students watching him in anticipation.

He cleared his throat. "You will note that Pope's translation of *The Odyssey*—"

Forty hands moved toward the quill pens sitting in their ink pots. "Wait." Byron held up his hand. "The dictation has not yet begun. For now, you are to listen."

The students dunked their quill pens back inside their ink-wells and turned their attention back to Byron. "In his translation," he continued, "Pope chose to use the Roman names for the deities of the Greek Pantheon."

One of the students raised her hand.

"Yes, Miss Williams."

"Why would Greek deities have Roman names at all?"

"Because the Romans adopted the Greek gods as their own

and renamed them."

Miss Williams's hand shot up again. "But why did Mr. Pope use their Roman names if *The Odyssey* is a Greek work?"

"To accommodate his audience."

More hands shot up. Byron squeezed the bridge of his nose. "Why isn't important. What's important—" he paused, trying to remember what he had wanted to say, "what's important is that you are able to identify the gods by both their Roman and their Greek names."

He gestured to the inkwells. "You may begin writing now." The students retrieved their pens. "The gods mentioned in the passages we read today are Jove, Minerva, Neptune, and—" He reached for his book, unable to declutter his mind enough to remember the other god it mentioned. He opened the book, and the letters swam before his eyes. It took him several minutes to regain his focus. "Mercury." He snapped the book shut. "Minerva is the Roman name for the goddess Athena, and Neptune is the Roman name for Poseidon." He paced the aisles as he spoke, giving cursory glances to the notebooks. "Mercury is Hermes, the messenger god, and Jove is, of course, Zeus, king of the gods."

Sweat collected on Byron's forehead. Try as he may, he could not get his mind off Violet and focus. Forgetting her was going to be more difficult than he had thought.

CHAPTER SEVENTEEN

Go from me. Yet I feel that I shall stand
Henceforward in thy shadow.

—Elizabeth Barrett Browning, "Sonnet VI"

"YOU'VE BEEN CRYING." Ottilie's observation sounded almost accusatory. She strode into Violet's room and shoved the door closed.

Violet slumped onto her bed.

"Will you at least tell me if there is anything I can do to help?" Ottilie perched on the edge of the mattress and eyed Violet. "Did something happen this morning before the lecture?"

Violet shook her head.

"Did he hurt you?" Ottilie's tone rose to a frantic, high pitch.

"No, of course not." Violet felt tears sting her eyes again. "But—"

Ottilie reached out and clasped Violet's hand.

"I have been such a fool. I let him sway me with tender words and gestures. He held my hand in the carriage on the way back from the gallery and gave me the impression that he cared for me. We confided in each other. He was so kind and gentle." Violet remembered with great shame how she'd clung to him when he had kissed her and how she had enjoyed it when he had caressed her breasts through the thin fabric of her dress.

"I heard not a word from him on Sunday. And then this morning, he avoided me before the lecture and spoke coldly to me when he arrived at class. I could feel that he wanted to distance himself from me." A sob escaped her throat. "It was as if he was embarrassed by our encounter."

Ottilie squeezed Violet's hand. "I am sorry."

Violet took a deep breath and wiped her eyes. "This is my fault, entirely. I should have known he was playing me for a fool. One minute he is kind and attentive, and the next, he is cold and distant. I should have expected this result."

"You mustn't blame yourself. Mr. Thomas is at least eight years your senior and your master. His behavior has been disgraceful. We ought to report this to Headmistress Briggs."

"No! Promise me that you will not breathe a word about this to the headmistress, or I fear I shall never be able to face her or anyone else at this institution again."

Ottilie dropped her gaze and let go of Violet's hand to pull at the fingertips of her gloves.

Violet stared at her. "Ottilie! You know how people talk. I will be disgraced and my reputation ruined. I'd lose my position, and then what would I do? I wouldn't even be suitable enough to be a governess."

"You needn't worry about losing your position. Headmistress Briggs is different. She doesn't think the same way others do."

"Headmistress Briggs may be enlightened, but she must live in the same world as the rest of us. Her students would not want their reputation tainted by mine, and I couldn't bear that. I want an education, and I want to help other women get one, too. That is more important to me than anything. I temporarily lost my head, that is all."

Ottilie nodded. "You are right."

Violet stood up and crossed her arms. "I will not run from him. Nor will I give up my place here. It is too important to me. So, there is nothing left for me to do but hold my head high and restore my dignity. I can be as cold and indifferent as he."

"That may be, but at the very least, you should insist on having a better chaperone than old Mrs. Ward."

"I cannot. Headmistress Briggs will wonder why."

Ottilie shook her head. "She should have provided more than one chaperone in the first place. Queen's College provides multiple chaperones at all lectures."

"I can take care of myself. I may look fragile on the outside, but do not think me soft and delicate inside. I have endured losses far more precious than Mr. Byron Thomas. I cry not for him but for my own stupidity and ignorance. I am ashamed, that is all."

"You have nothing to be ashamed for!"

"I do, Ottilie. I got swept up in some ridiculous romantic notions and so behaved badly and out of character. And I must—I *will*—take responsibility for my own actions."

A knock on the door silenced Violet.

"Who could that be?" Violet said in a whispered panic. "I cannot see anyone looking like this." She covered her swollen eyes with her hands.

"I'll answer it." Ottilie stood, smoothed out her dress, and stepped forward to pull open the door.

"Miss Hamilton! Is Miss Greyson in?" Violet recognized Nellie's voice.

"Yes, but she's indisposed at the moment, Nellie. May I help you?"

"There's a messenger downstairs. He's waitin' for Miss Greyson. Says it's urgent and that he must deliver the message to her in person." Violet dropped her hands to her lap and when Ottilie glanced over her shoulder, Violet shrugged. She had no idea what this was about.

"Thank you, Nellie. She'll be down shortly." Ottilie closed the door and turned to Violet. "I hope this is not Mr. Thomas playing more of his games with you."

"I don't know, but we will find out soon enough." Violet stood, grabbed her shawl, and threw it over her shoulders. "Let's go."

They tramped down the stairs and rushed across the hall to the main door of the building. As soon as Violet stepped outside, she recognized her aunt's coachman. Violet slowed her pace as she approached him. He bowed and smiled at her before handing her a sealed envelope.

Violet's heart hammered. Had something happened to her aunt? She turned away from the coachman to break the seal and read her message in private.

My Dearest Niece,

I regret to inform you that your uncle, Sir Richard Astyr, caught an illness while in India that weakened his heart. He is, alas, no more my husband. I am beside myself. Please come at once.

Lady Prudence Astyr (your loving aunt)

Violet stared at the paper as she digested the news. Her uncle was dead. She didn't feel any sense of loss or remorse about it; after all, she had barely known the man. But her aunt was asking for help, and she felt a strong sense of duty to assist her sole remaining blood relative. Violet folded the letter and placed it back in its envelope before turning to face the coachman.

She bit her lip. She needed to inform Headmistress Briggs before she could take leave, but her uncle was dead, and her aunt needed her now. She felt as if the world was spinning. So much had occurred within the last few hours, it seemed surreal.

"I hope there is nothing the matter." Ottilie's voice broke into Violet's thoughts.

Violet glanced at the coachman before answering. She was uncertain what had been revealed to the servants. "My aunt has received some distressing news, and she desires my help. I must go to her at once, but I need to inform Headmistress Briggs that I may be absent for several weeks."

"Several weeks! Will you be returning to Devonshire?"

"No, thankfully, I will not have to journey that far. My aunt lives in Mayfair."

"You have an aunt in Mayfair?" Ottilie's blue eyes widened. "You didn't mention that you had any relatives in London, let alone Mayfair."

"It is rather a long story," Violet said. "I promise to tell you everything one day, but right now, I need to send word to the headmistress and pack my things."

"Don't worry. I will inform Headmistress Briggs that you departed suddenly due to a family emergency." Ottilie extended a hand toward Violet. "You can tell me what it is you want me to say to her while I assist you with your packing."

"That will be of great help to me, thank you." Violet smiled and clasped Ottilie's hand. She turned to the coachman. "You may wait for me in the coach. I will need a few minutes to pack and ready myself."

He nodded. "Of course, miss."

"Will you at least allow me to call on you while you are away?" Ottilie asked as they walked back to Violet's room.

"Yes, of course, although I hope not to be gone from my studies for too long."

"I think it will do you good to get away from Mr. Thomas for a while."

Violet nodded and forced a smile, but her heart ached.

A RESTLESS SLEEP left Byron agitated and anxious in the morning. All night, his mind had been plagued by doubt and remorse at the memory of Violet's distress. Why had he thought it necessary to be so cold and cruel to her? Perhaps he could have handled things differently. His heart ached at the thought of her tears. He longed to hold her in his arms again and explain things to her. But he knew that, in the long term, cruelty would be kinder. She would grow to hate him, and then she would be free to give her heart to someone else. Back and forth, these thoughts spun in his mind until he no longer knew what he believed was best. Just one day ago, he had been certain of what actions he needed to take, and now, exhaustion and grief blurred his thinking and made him question himself over and over again.

He loathed getting out of bed, knowing that he had very little to look forward to and a lot to dread. Is this what the rest of his life would feel like?

Unable to face a tedious and drawn-out morning of teaching, he set his sixth formers the task of translating a long passage of *The Aeneid*. They worked diligently at it as he paced between the rows of desks, throwing cursory glances at their notebooks, his mind churning.

"Sir." William Taylor raised his hand.

"Is your translation complete, Taylor?" Byron snapped.

"No, sir, but—"

"Then put your hand down."

"But sir—"

This second interruption earned Taylor a thrashing on the arm from a prefect. The poor boy yelped like an injured pup, and a nugget of guilt pinched Byron. He had suffered under the ruthless cane as a child and secretly hated the practice of corporal punishment. Taylor's hand trembled as he returned to his translation, creating an inkblot on his page. The prefect raised his cane a second time, but Byron held up his hand to stop him from unloading it on the boy.

"That's not necessary, Phillips. Thank you."

He made a mental note to speak with Phillips after class and make it clear, once again, that he did not condone excessive force. He feared the boy had a sadistic streak in him, and if not stopped, he would become a tyrant, bullying his wife and children with his cane or worse, his fists as Byron's father had done. Still, he respected the system too much to reprimand a prefect in front of the others.

"Please, sir," a quivering voice sounded to his left, and Byron glanced down to see one of the younger students holding out an envelope to him. "A message for you, sir."

Byron frowned. He had not even noticed the boy entering the room, and he wondered how long the lad had been standing there, trying to get his attention. Then it dawned on him that poor Taylor had no doubt been trying to make him aware of the little messenger.

He took the envelope from the boy's trembling hand and saw that it was from Westminster Ladies' College. Inside was a short note from Headmistress Briggs requesting his presence in her office at five o'clock. Byron crumpled the envelope into a ball and swallowed the lump of fear that had risen in his throat. It had to have something to do with Violet. If the headmistress had wanted to talk about Amelia and the engagement, she would have summoned him to her home and not her office.

Had Violet spoken to the headmistress? No, she would not. He was certain of it. But what of Miss Hamilton? Perhaps she had reported what she had witnessed in the garden—a master kissing his student. Or, what if someone else witnessed him kissing Violet on college grounds? Violet's reputation with the other students and teachers would be ruined, and she was sure to be expelled.

The thought turned his blood to ice.

CHAPTER EIGHTEEN

When lovely woman stoops to folly,
And finds too late that men betray,—
What charm can soothe her melancholy,
What art can wash her guilt away?

—Oliver Goldsmith, "When Lovely Woman Stoops"

"NOT DEAD?" VIOLET gaped at her aunt. "Whatever do you mean? Your letter said that my uncle had died in India of a weak heart. That is why I came straight away. When I arrived yesterday evening, your lady's maid said that you were so distraught you'd taken to bed with a bottle of laudanum. I was worried sick all night."

Aunt Prudence lifted her chin. "I was indeed upset, and I had a terrible headache. The laudanum helps me sleep."

Violet sighed. "I am pleased to hear that Sir Richard is alive and well, I truly am, but I don't understand why you informed me otherwise. If you wanted to see me, you need only have asked."

"I do not recall saying that he had died," her aunt said haughtily. "I merely stated that he had a weak heart and was no longer my husband."

"But why would you say that when it is not true?" Violet worked to keep her patience in check.

"It *is* the truth. Sir Richard *does* have a weak heart, and he is no longer my true husband."

"I took leave of my position at Westminster Ladies' College so that I could support you in your mourning," Violet said, shaking her head, "and now you tell me that my uncle is living comfortably in India!"

Aunt Prudence blinked several times and then burst into a flood of tears. Violet rushed to her side. "I have long since suspected and have now confirmed," she said between gulps of breath, "that Sir Richard keeps a second wife in India."

"But that is bigamy!" Violet gasped.

"I do not mean that he has actually married another woman," she tutted, "but he lives with her in India as if she were his wife. That is why he spends so much time there and so little time here."

"How do you know this?"

"I hired one of those private investigator people and paid for his passage to India. Then when Sir Richard returned home three days ago, I confronted him with the evidence, and he did not deny it. Now, he has returned to India and left me quite alone." She dabbed her eyes with her lace handkerchief.

"How dare he treat you thus?" Anger swelled in Violet's chest. She clenched her fist, thinking as much of Byron's sins as her uncle's.

"Thank you." Aunt Prudence patted Violet's hand. "You are a great comfort to me—my dearest niece, my own sister's daughter. That is why I sent for you. I am not alone at all; you and I can be together now, and your uncle can no longer keep us apart."

"I shall visit you as often as possible," Violet reassured her. "And you may call on me as often as you like."

"Visit me? There will be no need for that when we are living together. Do you not see? With your uncle permanently in India, he will no longer object to you staying here with me."

Violet frowned. "But I cannot stay with you. I have residence at the college and responsibilities. I am training to become an educator there myself one day."

"Fiddlesticks! You are the niece of Lady Astyr, not a common schoolgirl. And certainly not a working woman! There will be no more need for that ladies' college nonsense."

Violet reached for her tea and tried to keep from losing her patience. "You misunderstand me. I want to go back to school, and I want to be a working woman today and every day."

"Ridiculous," Aunt Prudence said.

"It isn't ridiculous; it's true! Never in my life have I felt more at home than inside the walls of Westminster Ladies' College. Only in my dreams did I ever imagine such a place could exist where young women are free to learn just as young men do."

"Scandalous!" Aunt Prudence fanned her face with her handkerchief. "The classics, indeed! What good will knowledge of the classics do you when you are married? A man does not want a woman who can translate Homer and Virgil as well as he can. What use will that be to you as a wife and mother? No." She shook her head. "I will hear no more about such nonsense. We must think, instead, of the season ahead. We must prepare to introduce you to society. You will need new dresses, shoes, and—"

"Stop!" Violet said, "I will not need anything. I am three-and-twenty and far too old to be presented to society—nor do I wish to find a husband. I will be returning to Westminster Ladies' College, where I hope Headmistress Briggs will one day employ me as a teacher."

"I thought you were finished with that nonsense. Do you know that your headmistress's mother was a bluestocking and her husband an embezzler? Not to mention, her daughter has a rather questionable reputation. Do you want to be outside of polite society before you are even introduced to it, Violet?"

"That's naught but gossip. Mrs. Briggs isn't some lady of ill repute. She is an intelligent individual, highly respected by many, who believes in education and the empowerment of women."

Aunt Prudence turned her face from Violet's. "So, you mean to abandon me for that modern-day bluestocking and her radical school?"

"I will never abandon you. But I must be free to make my own choices." Violet paused as her aunt sniffed into her handkerchief. "I do not expect you to understand the choices I make in life, but I do ask that you respect them."

Aunt Prudence blinked at Violet through her tears. "Perhaps you are wiser than me. I followed every rule and made an excellent match, but it wasn't good enough."

"That is why women like Headmistress Briggs are so important. There are only a few of them, but they are brave and determined."

Violet shuddered. "You will not go back to that horrid institution right away, will you, Violet?" she asked. "Not so soon after Sir Astyr abandoned me in such a cruel fashion?"

Violet's heart sank at the prospect of staying in Mayfair for an indeterminate amount of time; nevertheless, she squeezed her aunt's hand and said, "Of course not. I will stay with you for as long as is necessary."

A KNOT OF dread lodged itself in Byron's throat as he entered Westminster Ladies' College and made his way to the headmistress's office.

"Come in," Headmistress Briggs called, in response to his knock.

He opened the door and balked. Ottilie Hamilton sat across from the headmistress's desk.

"Do take a seat, Mr. Thomas." The headmistress motioned to an empty seat next to Miss Hamilton.

He forced his legs to move and sat down.

Headmistress Briggs cleared her throat and seemed hesitant to speak, as if uncertain how to formulate her words. Byron felt as if he were a boy again, sitting across from his father, waiting for him to strike like Zeus throwing his lightning bolt down from the heavens on some mortal sinner below.

"Is something the matter?" he asked with feigned innocence.

"I am afraid so." Headmistress Briggs looked at him pointedly. "There has been an unfortunate incident, the consequences of which will affect you directly, I'm afraid."

"What is it?" He said, unwilling to let go of his show of ignorance.

"It involves Miss Greyson."

The banging of his heart reached his ears. He felt as though he might faint.

"She has been called away."

He frowned. He had not been expecting to hear that. He had been preparing to defend himself, but now his concern turned to Violet. "Has something happened?"

"It is her uncle. He has passed away. Miss Hamilton informs me that she left in a hurry earlier today. It seems that her aunt was quite distressed, and Miss Greyson did not specify how long she would be gone."

"I was not aware that she had an uncle or an aunt." Byron's mind clouded in confusion.

"Well, you would not be expected to know that. The important thing is that I have asked Miss Hamilton to fill in as your assistant until Miss Greyson returns. As you already know, she is quite the scholar."

"I see." His mind whirled with questions about Violet.

"I am sorry," Headmistress Briggs said. "I know how difficult it was for you to find an assistant of your liking. Try to remember that this situation is temporary. I am certain Miss Greyson will be back within a month."

A month? This was a blessing. By the time Violet returned, he would be married to Amelia, and she would accept the change with ease—having had some distance from him. He would not need to spend the coming weeks forcing himself to be cruel and cold in order to create distance. They would be able to remain friends and continue working together. It was for the best.

The only objection he had was to Miss Hamilton replacing Violet. He could not tolerate that.

Byron leaned forward and frowned as if deep in thought. "Does Miss Hamilton not already assist Mr. Raymond?"

"She does, indeed. But he has kindly agreed to go without an assistant for a few weeks in light of the fact that you have a busy month ahead with the wedding taking place in two weeks, during half term."

Byron swallowed.

"I hope you don't mind that I told Miss Hamilton the good news already. Rest assured she is the first outside the family to hear."

"Please accept my congratulations, Mr. Thomas," Miss Hamilton said. "I shall do my best to ease your workload in honor of this special occasion." A hint of anger bobbed on the surface of her words that chilled Byron.

She would write to Violet and tell her the news. And she would paint the worst possible picture of him. He would become a villain in Violet's eyes, and she would never return to Westminster Ladies' College. That was more than he could bear.

A knock on the door interrupted his thoughts.

"Enter," Headmistress Briggs called.

The door cracked open, and Headmistress Briggs's assistant appeared. "The milliner is here to see you."

"Oh, yes." She stood up. "Please excuse me. I will only be gone a moment. Do use this time to fill Miss Hamilton in on her duties, Mr. Thomas."

Byron waited for Headmistress Briggs to leave before addressing Miss Hamilton. "Do you know Miss Greyson's whereabouts? I should like to speak with her or write to her, if possible."

She narrowed her eyes. "Regarding your engagement to Miss Farthington?"

"As a matter of fact, yes, but that is none of your business."

Miss Hamilton glared at him. "Well, as it happens, I do not know where she has gone. She left in somewhat of a hurry by coach. I assume she went to Dartmoor, where her family resides."

She was lying. That much was obvious. He calmed himself

and forced himself to speak politely. "Please, Miss Hamilton, if you hear from her, will you let me know right away? I must have her address. I must write to her or see her and explain—"

"Explain why you violated her honor, and the next day became engaged to Miss Farthington?" She spoke in a low, angry whisper. "I do not think she will welcome any explanation you give. Have you not done enough? Can you not let her grieve her uncle in peace?"

"You do not know of what you speak," Byron ground out. "I had no intention of marrying Miss Farthington when—"

"So, you have deceived her as well as Miss Greyson?"

Byron rubbed the back of his aching neck. "The situation is complicated. I cannot explain it to you without betraying another's confidence. But I can assure you that I have deceived nobody, least of all Miss Greyson. And if you are truly her friend, you will provide me with her whereabouts as soon as you know them."

Miss Hamilton lifted her chin and looked straight ahead, ignoring Byron's plea.

They sat in silence and waited for Headmistress Briggs to return.

"Well, Mr. Thomas, have you made your new assistant aware of her duties?" The headmistress bustled back into her office and sat down.

Byron stood up. "Thank you for the offer, but I must decline the offer of Miss Hamilton's assistance."

She cocked her head as though she did not understand.

"Please do not trouble Mr. Raymond by taking away his assistant on my account. I do not anticipate this month being any busier than last month—unless you intend to involve me in the planning of the wedding, that is."

"Of course not." Headmistress Briggs smiled tightly. "My daughter wouldn't hear of it."

"Excellent, then we have nothing further to discuss, and I will take my leave." He bowed his goodbyes and strode out of the office.

CHAPTER NINETEEN

Bid me to weep, and I will weep,
While I have eyes to see;
And having none, yet I will keep
A heart to weep for thee.

—Robert Herrick, "To Anthea, Who May Command
Him Anything"

A MERRY TUNE drifted from the dining room into the hallway. Violet smiled, pleased to hear that her aunt's spirits had lifted. She only wished hers would lift too. After taking refuge in Mayfair for a week, it was time to pluck up the courage and return to college.

"There you are, Violet!" Aunt Prudence looked up from her breakfast. "I thought you were going to sleep all morning."

Violet glanced at the grandfather clock in the corner of the room. It read 10:05 a.m. She had slept late again.

"Come and sit down. You must eat a good breakfast. We have a busy day ahead of us."

Violet seated herself on one of the mahogany and blush velvet chairs surrounding the dining table. Sunlight filtered through a large, mullioned window and warmed the room, decorated in various pink and gold floral patterns. A boiled egg cradled in a porcelain cup awaited her.

A footman appeared at her side. "Tea, miss?"

"Thank you."

"Give her a slice of toast with marmalade and several slices of bacon and smoked herring. She cannot subsist on a boiled egg and tea. We have a busy day ahead."

Her aunt's words echoed Ottilie's opinions about her choice of breakfast and brought a smile to Violet's face. "What do you mean, we have a busy day ahead?"

"We must go shopping, my dear. You need an evening and ball gown, at the very least."

"You have already bought me too many new dresses," Violet protested. "I do not need—"

Aunt Prudence held up her hand to silence Violet. "Are you going to refuse me the pleasure of purchasing a few dresses for my dead sister's daughter? Especially when it's my only glimmer of pleasure during these dark days."

Violet sighed, picked up her spoon, and cracked her egg. She did not want to appear ungrateful, but she could not help feeling annoyed. She'd been lured back to Mayfair under false pretenses, and now her aunt seemed to be using her as a distraction from her troubles.

On the other hand, she pitied the woman. Her husband had controlled her, kept her from her family, and then abandoned her. But couldn't she see that was precisely why Violet needed to return to her studies?

Aunt Prudence resumed her humming, and Violet wondered at her cheerful mood. "You said Mama married for love and seemed to think that a bad idea. Did you not love Sir Richard when you married him?"

The woman's cheeks turned pink, and her eyes took on a wistful look. "I did. I thought him the most handsome man in the world. He looked so elegant in his lieutenant's uniform."

"And did you believe he loved you?" Violet picked up her teacup.

Her aunt shifted in her seat. "I believed he would grow to

love me after Elizabeth ran off with—your father."

"What?" Violet almost dropped her cup. Tea splashed onto the table, but she was too stunned to care. "Uncle *Richard* was engaged to Mama?"

Aunt Prudence exhaled. "It wasn't a love match. Our papa arranged the marriage after he discovered your papa was courting her during her stay with friends in Devonshire. He was furious and ordered her back to London. Then he arranged for a quick marriage to Sir Richard—his distant cousin and a military man he admired. Elizabeth pretended to comply and then eloped with your papa.

Violet narrowed her eyes in thought. "Is that why Papa was banished to a small parish on the moors?"

Her aunt tilted her head as if to consider this. "I do not know. It's very likely. Your grandfather was a powerful man, and their disobedience enraged him. He disinherited Elizabeth and never spoke to her again. I think he regretted it later, but he and our mama died in that terrible carriage accident before they could make amends."

Realization dawned as everything suddenly became clear to Violet. "So that is why Sir Richard despises us?"

"The rejection humiliated him. You can understand; he is a proud man. But my papa compensated him, and in the end, he was pleased enough to accept me and my hefty dowry." She shrugged. "I was young and foolish. I thought Sir Richard would appreciate my devotion to him and come to love me, but I don't believe he ever did."

Violet sat in stunned silence. Was anything in the world what it seemed to be? Or was everything tainted by deceit and lies? She thought of her parents. They did not own a fancy house with carriages and servants, but at least their love had been true.

"A message for you, Miss Greyson."

Violet turned, startled to see the butler standing beside her, holding a silver tray containing a single envelope and a silver letter opener. She picked up the envelope and immediately recognized the handwriting as Ottilie's. Using the letter opener, Violet freed her letter and read:

My dearest Violet:

Thank you for your letter and invitation to visit. Of course, I shall come and see you this afternoon. I miss you desperately and have much news. Headmistress Briggs asked me to take over your duties during your absence, but Mr. Thomas insists on doing things himself—thank goodness! I hope you are well, and I cannot wait to see you again.

Please offer my sincerest condolences to your aunt.

Yours, Ottilie

"What is it, dear?" Aunt Prudence craned her neck to see the contents of the letter.

Violet refolded it and placed it back inside its envelope. "A friend from the ladies' college. I need to meet with her today. I left in rather a hurry. I'm afraid the shopping will have to wait."

Aunt Prudence pursed her lips. "You stay here, my dear. I will venture out on my own. It is for the best since I am not sure we will agree on what material to purchase for your gowns. You seem to prefer dowdy colors, but the fashion today calls for much brighter hues. I will have Sara take your measurements after breakfast, and then I will set out directly."

"Nothing too extravagant, please. I won't wear anything that makes me look like a dress-up doll," Violet pleaded, knowing she would soon be brightly dressed, nonetheless.

VIOLET COULD NOT stop herself from rushing to the door and embracing her friend as soon as she heard Ottilie's voice.

"Thank you, Oliver. I will show Miss Hamilton to the parlor myself."

"Very well, miss. Shall I instruct Sara to bring in tea?"

"Please."

Oliver bowed and left them.

"Violet! How different you look! I can scarcely recognize you." Ottilie stared wide-eyed at Violet's pale blue dress. Violet shook her head. "Please, do not comment on it. My aunt insisted on buying me a new wardrobe. I can hardly move, encased in this ridiculous crinoline." Violet linked arms with Ottilie and walked her to the drawing room.

"I don't understand. Why the new dress? I thought you were in mourning for your uncle."

"I am not in mourning." Violet entered the parlor and led Ottilie to sit on a mustard yellow sofa. "As it turns out, my uncle is not dead."

"What? That is wonderful news. I am so relieved to hear it."

"It is not quite so wonderful. You see, my uncle is not physically dead, but he is as good as dead—at least, according to my aunt."

Ottilie frowned. "You are talking in riddles."

"He has decided to stay in India permanently," Violet said.

"And your aunt objects because she does not want to live in India?"

"No." Violet lowered her voice. "She objects because my uncle has other interests of the female variety that keep him in India."

Ottilie's eyes grew round as Violet's meaning became clear to her. "Oh, how awful! Men can be horrible. They have all the power. That is why I never want to get married."

"It *is* awful. And now, my aunt is leaning on me for comfort and dressing me up like a living doll. She is against my returning to school and instead wishes to marry me off to someone of her liking. She is out shopping for more dresses as we speak."

A knock on the door indicated tea had arrived. Sara entered with a tray of tea and cakes, and they waited for her to leave the room before pouring the tea and continuing their conversation. "On the subject of awful men—" Ottilie began.

Violet froze, her teacup poised at her lips. She returned it to its saucer. "Let's not speak of him. Please, I cannot bear it just now."

Ottilie fixed her eyes on Violet's. "I am afraid we must. Something has happened. And I am sorry to be the bearer of bad news, but as your friend, I cannot wait for you to hear it from another source."

"Is it Byron? Is he injured? Unwell?" Fear shot through Violet's veins.

"Oh no," Ottilie said, "He is quite well, indeed."

"Then go on," Violet said with a sigh. "Whatever it is, it cannot be that bad."

Ottilie leaned forward and clasped Violet's hands in hers. "Mr. Thomas and Miss Farthington are set to be married at the end of this month."

Violet slipped her hands out of Ottilie's grasp and folded them on her lap. "Is it official?"

Ottilie nodded. "Headmistress Briggs told me herself when she asked me to take over your duties."

"She told you this last week?"

"I wanted to tell you sooner, but I thought you were mourning your uncle and did not wish to add to your upset. I am so sorry, Violet. He has used you very badly."

Violet felt the air drain from her lungs. She'd secretly hoped that upon her return, Byron would apologize and give her a reasonable explanation for his cold behavior. Despite herself, she believed—hoped—that he loved her. But now that he was to be married, her hopes were shattered. She rubbed her forehead in confusion. "The end of the month? So soon! He must have been engaged to her when we—" Violet covered her face with her hands. *Byron must have committed to Miss Farthington the day after their trip to the museum. That explained why he'd avoided her and behaved so coldly toward her. How can it be that I misjudged a person's character so badly? Have I no awareness at all? Am I truly so naive?*

Ottilie caressed her friend's back, trying to offer what comfort she could. "After we met with Headmistress Briggs, he dared to tell me that he never intended to marry Miss Farthington. He said the situation was complicated, and he could not reveal the details without violating another's privacy. Then, he dared to ask me to provide him with your address. I refused. I told him that I did not know your current whereabouts."

"I don't think I shall ever be able to return to school and face him again," Violet said.

"You must! Miss Farthington may have taken Mr. Thomas from you, but do not let her take your education and future. You must put this behind you."

"But how will I keep from feeling shamed and belittled each time I see him?"

"I have an idea," Ottilie said. "But you will need courage."

"WHY DO YOU sit in the study drinking brandy with the curtains drawn instead of joining the rest of our guests?" Amelia marched into the library and stood in front of Byron's chair.

"Why should you care what I do?" he said and took another sip of brandy.

"I care because my friends and family will attend the wedding, and I do not wish for you to spoil everything and embarrass me. What do you think people will say if my intended stands on the altar and glowers at me, looking and smelling like a street urchin from St. Giles?"

"What should I care what your friends think?"

Amelia stamped her foot. "So, you will embarrass Mama and Mr. Briggs? Do not imagine you will become headmaster if you do that!"

Byron slammed his glass down onto the rosewood table that stood beside his chair. Amelia jumped. "I have already agreed to marry you, so why do you continue to plague me, Amelia?"

"*Agreed* to marry me?" Amelia smirked. "If it weren't for my condition, any man would consider himself lucky to marry me."

"So why don't you marry the father of your child? Or doesn't he want you?"

Amelia narrowed her eyes. "*You* are the father of my child."

"An immaculate conception, was it?" He retrieved his brandy. "Tell me, why doesn't he want you? Is he married?"

Amelia's face hardened.

"That's it, isn't it? You bedded a married man—you harpy!"

She flew at him and swiped his cheek with her nails, scratching the surface of his skin. Byron caught her wrist. "You cannot stomach the idea that a man exists on this earth who does not worship you for your beauty, can you?"

"So, you think I am beautiful?" Amelia sank to the ground between his knees.

Byron released her wrist and turned his head. He wasn't prepared to play her games.

"Do you not desire me?" Amelia crept closer to him. "I am to be your wife after all."

"In name only." Byron kept his face averted.

She leaned closer to him and ran her hand up his thigh. He wanted to push her away, but the brandy fuzzed his brain and made him sluggish. Her face hovered inches from his, and the delicate floral scent of her French perfume added to his intoxication.

"Why do you turn your face from me?" she whispered. "Look at me and tell me that I am not beautiful. Tell me that you do not desire me."

Byron turned and, in doing so, brushed against her soft red lips. He closed his eyes and thought of the kisses he'd shared with Violet. The ache of loneliness and yearning for Violet overwhelmed him. Amelia pressed her lips against his neck, and, thinking of Violet, he let out a low moan.

CHAPTER TWENTY

I clenched my brows across
My blue eyes greatening in the looking glass,
And said, 'We'll live, Aurora! we'll be strong.
The dogs are on us–but we will not die.'
—Elizabeth Barrett Browning, "Aurora Leigh"

A FASHIONABLE AND sophisticated young lady stared back at Violet from the oval-shaped, full-length mirror that graced the corner of Aunt Prudence's dressing room. Violet ran her hands over the smooth, royal blue silk of her gown and let them glide down the sides of her waist, which looked tiny above the hooped skirt of her dress. Her hair, styled by Elsie's skilled hands and decorated with sparkling pins, rested in an elegant chignon at the nape of her neck. Turning her head from side to side, she stared in awe at the sapphire pendant that graced her pale neck and seemed to transform it into something quite elegant. What an enormous difference an expensive dress and a beautiful piece of jewelry made to one's countenance, she thought. Yet, she could not imagine dressing this way every day. The tight bodice and balloon-like skirt, held up by a massive whale-bone crinoline, constricted her movements and made her feel rather foolish. How did a woman think clearly in such a contraption?

Perhaps that was the point.

"You look perturbed." Ottilie appeared in the mirror behind Violet and fiddled with one of her dangling emerald earrings. She looked effortlessly exquisite in a green and white lace-trimmed gown. "Are you having second thoughts?"

"I was just thinking how lucky I am not to have grown up rich like my mama."

Ottilie laughed. "Really?"

"I should hate to be stuffed into one of these dresses every day and forced to attend balls with the sole purpose of attracting a husband."

"Was life so very less constricting on Dartmoor? Did you not have to fill your days working around the house?"

"There was always work to do, but hardly a day went by that I didn't muddy my boots roaming outdoors." She breathed in deeply. "I miss the fresh air."

"It sounds wonderful." Ottilie took a seat on a pink-cushioned ottoman next to an ornate white dressing table. "Then, you haven't changed your mind about this evening? You are certain you wish to go forward with this?"

Violet rested her hands on her stomach to quiet the storm that brewed inside her. "I must," she said. "I cannot stay away from my studies any longer. Mr. Thomas is my schoolmaster and an excellent one at that, so I have no choice but to smile and congratulate him on his pending nuptials."

"Is that all?"

"And perhaps—" She turned to face Ottilie. "Perhaps I will leave tonight's gathering with some answers."

"Violet, do not torture yourself looking for explanations when there are none to be had that will satisfy you."

"I must. I've been over and over everything in my mind, and I still cannot understand what happened. It has only been three weeks since our outing to the National Gallery—since he—" She closed her eyes. "Yet tonight, he celebrates his engagement to Miss Farthington. And next week, he will be her husband."

Ottilie stood up, walked to Violet, and placed a hand on her shoulder. "You mustn't give it a moment's further thought. Mr. Thomas is a master manipulator who is skilled in doublespeak. I learned this morning that the situation with Miss Farthington is indeed complicated and a lot worse than it appears to be. Trust me; you want no part of Mr. Thomas or his explanations."

"What do you mean?" Violet tensed, bracing herself for more bad news.

"I am afraid the answer to that question will only distress you further. Can you not accept my word?"

"Of course, I do. I only seek to understand."

Ottilie paused as if taking the time to carefully consider her words before speaking. "I did not want to trouble you with this, but I see now that it is necessary as it will help you understand Mr. Thomas's true nature. Then, perhaps you will resolve to forget him."

"It cannot be as terrible as you say, surely," Violet said, fearing the opposite.

Ottilie inhaled deeply and closed her eyes as if she needed to gather her mental strength to say what came next. She breathed out and clasped Violet's hand. "I heard something from Nellie."

"From Nellie?" Violet withdrew her hand from Ottilie's. "The gossip you told me to ignore?"

"I know." Ottilie held up an open palm. "Trust me; I know. But this seemed too important to ignore, and, well, I just had an inkling that it might be true."

A hollow feeling settled in Violet's stomach. "Go on," she said.

Ottilie pressed her lips together and then started to speak in a gentle voice. "According to Nellie, the night before Miss Farthington and Mr. Thomas announced their engagement, there was a family row. It involved a lot of screaming and crying—mostly coming from Miss Farthington. Later that same evening, Mr. Thomas arrived, and the shouting started afresh. They were carelessly loud, and, well, the servants overheard Headmistress Briggs declare that Miss Farthington was with child." Ottilie paused. "Mr. Thomas's child."

"Oh, my Lord." The air seemed to vanish from Violet's lungs. "It cannot be true. Surely it is only idle gossip."

"I'm sorry, Violet. Ordinarily, I would agree with you and dismiss it as gossip, but it does explain the speed of this wedding."

"There must be some other explanation. How can it be that I misjudged a person's character so badly? Have I no awareness at all? Am I truly so naive?"

"Don't be too harsh on yourself. 'Reason and love keep little company', remember."

"Well, I have certainly acted the fool and proven Shakespeare right."

"But all that will change tonight. This evening, you will prove that you are no Helena, and you will be no man's spaniel." She linked her arm in Violet's. "Come, let's fetch our coats. Our carriage awaits."

"YOU'RE DRUNK." AMELIA scowled.

"Quite." Byron smirked. He had consumed enough brandy to ensure he remained numb for the entire evening.

"Come now." Mr. Briggs placed a hand on Byron's shoulder. "It is the man's engagement party. He has every reason to celebrate." He patted Byron on the back.

"Most definitely," Byron said, eager for another glass of brandy.

"There's Mr. Chapman, one of our trustees. Allow me to introduce you."

Byron followed Mr. Briggs across the crowded room. Once upon a time, he lived to impress the trustees of St. James's Academy, but now he cared little for these people. He feigned interest as Mr. Chapman prattled on and tried his best to keep his gaze steady as his mind wandered.

"What say you about that, Mr. Thomas?"

He turned his mind back to the conversation and furrowed his brow. "About what, sir?"

As Mr. Chapman opened his mouth to repeat the question, Byron lifted his gaze in drunken disinterest and scanned the room. He focused his eyes on Miss Hamilton, who had entered the room with a companion. He tried to follow the two women with his eyes as they moved through the crowd. Miss Hamilton's companion was petite and had Violet's alabaster skin. She wore a blue dress that exposed her neckline and shoulders. His heartbeat rose to a crescendo. *Could it be Violet? No, she was in Devonshire mourning her uncle, was she not?*

His heart sank. Even if she wasn't in mourning, Violet was far too stubborn to wear something so colorful and fashionable. The thought made him smile. Then again, Violet had surprised him more than once in the past. Curiosity propelled him forward, and he started moving toward the two women.

"Are you leaving us already?" Mr. Chapman inquired. "I am still waiting to hear your thoughts on the matter."

Byron inched forward, too focused on not losing sight of the women to acknowledge Mr. Chapman's question.

"You must excuse him, sir." The embarrassment in Mr. Briggs's voice was evident. "Mr. Thomas is quite distracted tonight in light of all the guests he must attend to."

Byron moved in the direction of Miss Hamilton and her companion with a singular focus, ignoring the guests who tried to greet or congratulate him as he weaved past them. He stopped a foot or so behind the women as they stood conversing with two other guests. He gazed at the pale skin on the back of the petite young woman's neck and shoulders, exposed by the sloping cut of her dress, and he knew he'd found Violet.

She must have sensed someone's presence behind her because she turned. Their eyes met, and she looked at him with cool indifference. Still, there was no mistaking her for another now. Only Violet could be the owner of those oceans of wisdom.

How different she looked without her high-necked somber black dress, a pile of notebooks, and ink-smudged fingers. He shifted his gaze to the smooth, pale skin on her throat and remembered a time, not long ago, when he'd worked his kisses up the length of her neck to her mouth and down again.

An exquisite sapphire pendant encased in gold glistened at the base of her neck.

It must cost a fortune. Where did she get an expensive piece like that? It had to have been a gift from someone very wealthy—a man, no doubt. Rage coursed through his veins.

Violet turned back to her companions and whispered something to Miss Hamilton. Byron found that he could not move or avert his gaze. Her honey-colored hair, adorned with winking sapphire pins, rested in a thick coil on the nape of her neck. She linked arms with Miss Hamilton, and together they moved farther into the crowd. Byron started to follow, but Amelia's voice pierced the air and fastened him in place like a pinned moth stopped mid-flight. "Here you are, Mr. Thomas! I have been searching for you everywhere."

Byron turned. Amelia stood with a couple he had never met before.

"Allow me to introduce Monsieur and Madame L'Strang from Paris."

The man had a haughty face with deep-set brown eyes, a sharp nose, and thin lips. His wife stood in his shadow, silent, and with a pinched look.

"At last! The professor himself." Monsieur L'Strang emphasized the word "professor" in a condescending tone.

Byron acknowledged the man's greeting with a slight nod while scanning the crowd for Violet. He wasn't in the mood for idle conversation.

But feeling Amelia's glare, he sighed inwardly and forced himself to feign interest in the French couple. "You have traveled from France to be here for the wedding next week, I presume?"

"Of course. We would not miss it." Monsieur L'Strang

glanced at Amelia suggestively, which heightened Byron's senses.

"And you will return to France directly after the wedding?"

"We will stay a few weeks. And why not?" Again, he looked at Amelia, although he addressed Byron. "There is much to do in London, no?"

Amelia tipped her head to the side and smiled flirtatiously at him.

Byron glanced at Madame L'Strang, who had averted her gaze to the floor.

"How did you and your husband meet Amelia, Madame L'Strang?"

The woman looked up and glanced at her husband before speaking. "My husband is Amelia's music teacher. She stayed with us for three months in Paris."

Oh, yes. L'Strang. The music master.

"They were so kind to me—inviting me to parties and introducing me to people. We all became such dear friends." Amelia exchanged another intimate glance with Monsieur L'Strang, and Byron thought he saw Madame L'Strang wince. He could not blame the woman. He knew Amelia well enough to ascertain that she was Monsieur L'Strang's lover and that she had done little to hide that fact from his wife. No doubt the child she carried belonged to the swine. He wasn't jealous, merely irritated that he had allowed himself to be manipulated into marrying Amelia—all for the sake of protecting the snake that stood before him. Suddenly, he felt suffocated by their presence, and as he spotted Violet at the far end of the room, strode off without saying another word.

CHAPTER TWENTY-ONE

With anger, now,
And like an archer, I have let these arrows
Fly at your heart, since you torment me so—
And you will not outrun their hot pain.

—Sophocles, "Antigone"

DEVOID OF PEOPLE and faintly illuminated by the gas lamps on the street outside its walls, the garden seemed a peaceful oasis to Violet. She treaded across the grass and made her way to a bench in a darkened corner, grateful for the opportunity to render herself invisible. She sat down and inhaled the cool night air, hoping it would ease the burning in her chest.

How could he be so callous, she wondered. When their eyes had met earlier, Byron had not even greeted her. In fact, he'd looked confused and angry to see her. No doubt he was upset that she'd intruded upon his happiness. Perhaps he'd hoped she would conveniently disappear from his life forever. Her chest tightened.

Why had she tortured herself by coming here? Ottilie had suggested that she face Byron sooner rather than later if she intended to return to the college. And she'd convinced herself that she was strong enough to do so. But seeing him with his soon-to-be-wife, surrounded by loved ones gathered to celebrate their happy union, proved to be too much for her to bear.

They made a striking couple, and it made sense that Byron had chosen Amelia. He would be headmaster of St. James's—and Amelia—Violet shuddered. What if she were to take a sudden interest in the college? She would certainly inherit the school from her mother one day. Violet wrapped her arms around herself. *I have no future in a place that will one day belong to Amelia Farthington.* Tears slid down her cheeks. All her hopes and dreams lay shattered before her. Once again, she'd lost everything dearest to her heart. And once again, she was left feeling utterly bereft.

BYRON SPENT SEVERAL minutes searching for Violet before stepping outside and disappearing into the shadows of the garden. He was desperate to escape the crowded room. He needed silence, space to breathe, and time to think.

Seeing Violet again had rendered him speechless. No one had told him that she'd returned to London. Yet, she had returned— not in her usual mourning clothes but looking radiant and dressed as he'd never seen her dressed before. What did it all mean? He'd thought he had lost her forever. But now, the gods had intervened and provided him with a second chance. Thankfully, he was not yet married to Amelia, and the presence of her pompous, pale-faced French lover convinced him that he should never have agreed to the union. The position of headmaster at St. James's was a lucrative one, but that, together with all of Briggs's money, could no longer convince him to sacrifice his second chance at happiness.

Anger rushed through his veins as he thought of Monsieur L'Strang's sneering smile. *What a fool Amelia must think I am to flaunt her lover in my face. The two of them are smug with deception. Do they think they can browbeat me the way they have Madame L'Strang? How she must despise her husband—repugnant man.* Byron gritted his teeth. *I will not marry Amelia and be a father to that bedswerver's child! To think I forsook Violet and my own happiness only to be a puppet dangling at the end of Miss Amelia Farthington's strings. I must have been mad!*

He strode forward into the darkness, so consumed by his anger that he almost lashed out when a body appeared out of nowhere and hurtled into him. Then he caught sight of a dress flying backward and pale arms windmilling in an attempt to regain balance. Instinctively, he reached out to grab one of the flailing arms.

"What are you doing out here in the dark?" Byron snapped as he pulled the lady to her feet.

"I might ask you the same thing," she retorted.

Byron turned rigid with shock. "Violet?" He peered at her in the dim light.

She stiffened, and Byron could sense the mental wall she'd constructed to keep him out. "The same as you, I expect. I came outside for a little air." Her tone remained cool and distant. "Now, if you will excuse me, Mr. Thomas, I think it is time for me to leave this party."

"Wait! Please, Violet. I wish to speak with you."

She paused but kept a noticeable distance from him.

"Where have you been these past weeks? I have been desperate to speak with you. Miss Hamilton said she did not know your whereabouts."

"Why should my whereabouts concern you, Mr. Thomas? I informed Headmistress Briggs that I would be absent due to a family crisis, and she arranged for Miss Hamilton to cover my duties, did she not?"

"I wasn't concerned about your duties, Violet. I wanted to talk to you; I wanted to explain things."

"Explain things? Such as why you led me to believe you cared for me? Or why you kissed me when you were planning to marry Miss Farthington?"

"I was not planning to marry her. I did not—*do not* love her."

"Yet here we are celebrating your upcoming nuptials, a short week before your wedding."

Byron moved a step closer. "Things occurred that were beyond my control. Things you do not understand."

"Unfortunately, I think I understand all too well."

The heat of her anger against the cold night air stunned him. In desperation, he reached for her arm and pulled her toward him. "You must listen to me. I do not love Amelia. They coerced me into proposing, but it is not too late to change things."

Violet struggled to free herself from his grip, "Let me go! I've heard enough lies from you. What is it you want from me? To be your final conquest before you wed? Do you wish to leave me unwed and with child, too?"

He released her as suddenly as if her skin had scorched him.

"So, it is true, then?" she said.

Byron stared at her. His mind buzzed with unanswered questions.

How does she know? Who could have told her? Someone in Briggs's house must have talked. Perhaps one of the servants? Or perhaps Amelia herself. If people believe I am the father of Amelia's unborn child, they will expect—nay, demand—that I do what's right. And there will be no escaping marriage after all.

"Well, Mr. Thomas?"

He opened his mouth to speak but found that he was unable to formulate a response. His head throbbed, and his thoughts scrambled out of his brain's reach.

"Is it true?" Violet asked.

"The child isn't mine; I swear to you."

"How do you know?"

"It's impossible, that's why."

"You never laid with her?"

Startled by her directness and demand for transparency, Byron opened his mouth to speak but could not form the words to explain. The unwanted, blurred image of Amelia sitting on top of him in the study flashed in his mind. He could not lie to her, so he said nothing.

"Right, I see." Violet's voice trembled.

Byron's throat constricted with pain. He'd underestimated Amelia. She'd used his weaknesses against him so that he could never again say that he hadn't lain with her before their wedding. And now, his weakness hurt Violet, and he felt like the most wretched bastard on earth.

He reached for her, but she wrenched away from him. "You have no business touching me! You never had."

Her words sliced through him and tore out his insides. Like a man drawn and quartered, he watched, paralyzed with pain, as she disappeared into the house.

CHAPTER TWENTY-TWO

A STROLL ALONGSIDE Hyde Park's Serpentine wasn't nearly as cathartic as a solo trek across Dartmoor's rugged and expansive moorlands; nonetheless, Violet welcomed the distraction. Despite Ottilie's questions about what had happened at the party the previous week, Violet had not shared the details of her encounter with Byron, nor would she admit that it was the deciding factor in her resolution to leave Westminster Ladies' College.

"I'm going to miss you," Ottilie said. "I do wish you'd reconsider."

"I'm only going to Harley Street; we shall see each other all the time. I promise."

"I know, but it won't be the same. I shall grieve the absence of our late-night teas, amongst other things."

Violet smiled, warmed by the idea that someone cared enough to grieve the loss of her company. "I'm going to miss that too. But Queen's College is a fine institution. And I'll be getting the training I need to open my own school one day. I won't begin until next term, of course, but I can keep up with my studies on my own until then."

Ottilie sighed. "It seems your mind is firmly made up."

"It is. I think an Anglican college will better suit me. My father was an Anglican minister, after all." She swallowed. "Perhaps the grief of his death made me lose my way. I've been going down the wrong path, and I must set myself right."

"Do you mean that you no longer wish to associate with dissenters and radicals like myself?"

"Of course not." Violet gave her friend's arm a squeeze. "It is not you or anyone else who has led me astray. But I must question my behavior of late. How is it that I fell so easily under Mr. Thomas's spell? How is it that I jeopardized my virtue, my integrity, and my position at the college? It makes me ashamed to think of it."

"You are too harsh on yourself." Ottilie steered Violet toward a bench at the edge of the walking path. "Because you're a good and honest person, you believe in people and trust them to be good and honest too, but unfortunately, some are not. The failure is theirs, not yours."

They sat down, and Violet tried to enjoy the warm spring rays, but she was too distracted. "I am afraid the failure is mine. I spent my life reading and studying in isolation, yet I thought myself ready for adult life—ready for London. In reality, I knew little of how the world works. You tried to warn me, but I refused to listen."

"Your words prove one thing—that you are human. At least you are capable of experiencing deep feelings, unlike the cold-hearted Mr. Thomas."

Violet fell silent and gazed at the rippling waters of the Serpentine. She remembered the expression of agony on Byron's face when he told her about the death of his wife and child. Had all that been an act? Had it all been to rouse her sympathy so that she would succumb to his kisses and caresses? How far would she have let things go if Ottilie had not spotted them in the garden and rescued her? Would she have been as foolish as the young Moll Flanders? Violet grimaced, remembering her scathing and self-righteous criticism of Defoe's protagonist. How Byron must smirk at the memory. That is, if he thought of her at all.

Tears pricked her eyes. The pain, still an open wound, threatened to overwhelm her again.

"Come," Ottilie said gently, "I think it is time we make our way back to Mayfair before the hordes come out to promenade."

They stood, and Ottilie linked her arm in Violet's as they stepped forward. Then she stopped abruptly. "Is that not Miss Farthington and Mr. Thomas strolling toward us?"

"What?" Violet peered at the approaching couple, her heart screaming at the thought of coming face to face with Byron. Miss Farthington wore a fuchsia dress that exposed her slim white shoulders, cinched her tiny waist, and ballooned around her torso thanks to the fashionably wide crinoline beneath. She carried an open parasol, white in color, and walked arm in arm with a gentleman—who, Violet noticed, was not Byron!

"Who is the gentleman with her? He is far too tall to be Mr. Thomas," Ottilie said.

"I'm not sure." Violet squinted at the pair. "I think I recognize him as one of the gentlemen from the engagement party. Perhaps he is a relation of hers."

"Well, we will soon find out." Ottilie stepped forward, pulling Violet with her.

"What on earth are you doing? I do not wish to engage in pleasantries with Miss Farthington."

"What else can we do? It would be rude to turn our backs and pretend not to have seen her."

"I do not particularly care whether or not Amelia Farthington thinks me rude," Violet snapped.

But Ottilie paid her no heed and pulled Violet into the couple's path. Amelia clung to the man's arm and gazed up at him with an expression of adoration. He returned her gaze and angled his body close. They were so focused on each other that they did not even notice Violet and Ottilie.

"Miss Farthington!" Ottilie stepped into Amelia's path, feigning surprise to see her. "How wonderful to see you so close to the date of your nuptials. I must thank you for the lovely party last week."

Amelia blinked at Ottilie as though she had no idea who she was. Then her gaze shifted toward Violet, and she smirked. "Of course. You two are helpers at Mother's little school. How sweet that you attended the party; I am pleased you enjoyed yourselves."

Violet's stomach tightened at the disparaging way in which Amelia referred to the ladies' college.

"Amelia, would you be so kind as to introduce me to these beautiful young ladies?" The man spoke with a heavy French accent and stared openly at Ottilie.

Violet and Ottilie exchanged a glance, mutually acknowledging the lechery of the man and the inappropriate way in which he had used Miss Farthington's Christian name in public.

"Of course." Amelia's dark eyes narrowed into slits. She turned to Violet as if wanting to deny Ottilie's existence. "This is Miss Greyson; she is Mr. Thomas's assistant, I believe."

The man glanced at Violet and acknowledged her with a quick nod. Then his gaze returned to Ottilie. "And who is this lovely creature?"

"Miss—" Amelia paused as if searching her memory for some obscure corner in which she had stored Ottilie's name.

"Hamilton," Ottilie said.

"That's correct. Miss Hamilton," Amelia said.

"I am quite certain it is correct." Ottilie gave Amelia a tight smile. "It has not changed since the day of my birth."

"You are not married?" The Frenchman's face took on a lascivious expression.

"I do not believe we have been introduced to this gentleman." Ottilie kept her eyes fixed on Amelia.

Amelia cleared her throat. "Miss Greyson, Miss Hamilton, I would like you to meet Monsieur L'Strang. He is my music instructor and dear friend from France." Amelia glanced adoringly at her companion.

Again, Violet exchanged a look with Ottilie, silently expressing her surprise. Amelia must have noticed because she added, "He and his wife have come for the wedding celebrations."

"How wonderful!" Ottilie said. "And will Madame L'Strang be joining you soon?"

"She is resting after all the festivities," Monsieur L'Strang said. "Too much noise and activity give her a 'headache'."

"I understand. And Mr. Thomas? Is he resting, too?"

"He was called away on a family matter this morning," Amelia interjected. "His father is gravely ill."

Violet let out an involuntary gasp, and Amelia shot her a hard look.

"I do hope you will not have to postpone the wedding," Ottilie said.

"Yes, we must. Mr. Thomas insisted on going to his father's house in Canterbury, even though he is greatly inconveniencing our guests." Amelia fluttered her eyelids at Monsieur L'Strang. "You will stay longer, won't you, Monsieur? You will not leave me to get married all on my own?"

Violet frowned.

"But of course, I will stay. Why not?" He eyed Ottilie. "After all, England has such beauty to offer a man, no?"

Amelia slipped her arm out of Monsieur L'Strang's and moved away from him in an apparent sulky protest. "May we go now? I am feeling a little unwell myself."

"So soon?" Monsieur L'Strang kept his eyes on Ottilie. "If we must." He reached for Ottilie's gloved hand and forced his kiss upon it. She snatched it away from him as if his lips were coated in snake's venom. He smiled, clearly eager to accept the challenge of such a difficult conquest. "Good day, Mademoiselle; it was enchanting to meet you." Then he turned to Violet and nodded before taking Amelia's arm again.

"That was most odd," Violet said as the pair strolled away. "She did not seem at all concerned about Mr. Thomas or his father. And she clung to that Frenchman as if he were the man to whom she was engaged. Did you notice how he stared at you? It was most disquieting. And that kiss on your hand…"

"It was more than disquieting," Ottilie said. "It was disgusting. After that encounter, I can say with certainty that something is thoroughly rotten in Denmark."

✦

HIS FATHER'S IMPENDING death brought only one thought to Byron's mind:

At last, he is doing something for me.

Byron stood at the gates of his childhood home—a sprawling stone mansion located a little over a mile outside the market village of Canterbury—and shuddered at the thought of stepping inside. Even his father's dying request would not have been enough to force his return to this mausoleum. As it happened, the request had come as a reprieve. He'd been desperate for a quick escape from his impending nuptials. And facing his father seemed a far better option than facing the reality of marriage to Amelia Farthington.

"Master Byron!" his father's long-suffering housekeeper greeted him at the door. "How you have grown!" Her plump face and periwinkle blue eyes brightened as she looked him up and down.

"Hello, Bessie." Byron smiled at the woman with genuine warmth. She was the only person besides his mother to show him kindness during his childhood.

Bessie ushered him inside. "Do come out of the cold and let me get a proper look at you." She dabbed her eyes. "I thought we'd never see you again."

"I wish the circumstances were better," Byron lied. He stepped inside and shivered. The decrepit mansion reeked of painful memories. "How is he?"

"Very frail but quieter now, thank the blessed Lord. When his illness first started some months ago, he would rage like a caged lion." Bessie shook her head. "He turned to drink to dull the pain, but it only made him rage more. Many priceless artifacts lay smashed, I'm afraid."

"Nothing too out of the ordinary, then." Byron patted Bessie on the shoulder. "It sounds as if little has changed since my departure for Cambridge."

"Oh, Master Byron, you always did know how to bring a smile to my face."

"I am pleased to hear it, Bessie." Byron glanced at the winding staircase in the middle of the foyer and sighed. "I suppose I should go up and see him directly."

"Surely you wish to get settled first. I've made up your old room. Where is your suitcase?" She scanned the area near Byron's feet.

"I'll be staying in town."

Bessie pressed her palm to her cheek and shook her head. "But this is your home, Master Byron."

"No, Bessie, you know as well as I do that it is not." The happiest day of Byron's life was the day his father sent him to school. Harsh as boarding school could sometimes be with its rules, thrashings, and bullies, it was a respite compared to this place.

Bessie blinked as if to stave off further tears. "Well, you must be hungry after your journey. I asked Cook to fix you some custard pudding. Those were your favorite when you were a lad, remember?"

"Of course, I do. Thank you." A smile played on Byron's lips as he recalled how Bessie would comfort him by sneaking custard pudding into his room after he had been whipped and sent to bed without supper for some trivial offense. His father's anger had always been palpable and could be roused by something as insignificant as the accidental drop of a quill. Whatever the cause, it had always resulted in a harsh thrashing for Byron. He would love nothing more than to take refuge in the kitchen with a plate of custard comfort, but he knew that he needed to get the unpleasant task of facing his father out of the way as soon as possible.

He glanced at Bessie. "I will come directly to the kitchen after seeing him. I promise." Then he made his way up the staircase feeling as weighed down as Sisyphus. He had no idea why his father wanted to see him now. He'd disowned and disinherited him years ago when he'd married Olivia and refused to return home to join his father's business. Byron had been adamant about keeping his new bride away from Canterbury. He would not subject her to his father's cruelty and so had taken a job teaching instead.

He shrank inwardly as he ascended the narrow, twisting staircase. With each step, the scuffle of his shoes against the stone infused him with loneliness. The unforgiving cold walls and hard floors served as a reminder of his boyhood isolation. He'd spent every dreaded school holiday pining for his dead mother whose lifeless image, lying beside the bundled corpse of his stillborn brother, remained etched in his mind. His father's cruelty had killed them both, and Byron's tears had only served to inflame the brute's temper. *"Stop your wailing, Milksop. I should have left you to the wolves like the Spartans would have done. You make me ashamed."*

He shook the memory from his mind and squared his shoulders before knocking on his father's chamber door. He was a man now, and he'd shown his father a long time ago that he would no longer stand to be bullied.

The door creaked open, and a hunched figure came into view. Bitter anger filled Byron's throat. Joseph, his father's valet, and faithful string puppet, gazed up at him and curled his lip.

"Who is it, Joseph?" He heard his father's feeble call. "Is it him?"

"It is sir."

"Joseph," Byron said curtly.

"Master Byron," Joseph rasped and scooted back as Byron stepped into the room. He heard the door click shut behind him and felt a momentary panic as his gaze shifted to his father. The man, whom he had always perceived as a Goliath, now lay like a withered leaf in his palatial bed.

His father lifted a shriveled hand in his direction. Byron hesitated before moving forward. The thought of touching that hand with the yellowing skin repulsed him. He neared the bed but stopped short of stepping within reach. As if to save face, his father swung his hand toward Joseph in one angry motion and barked, "Chair!"

Joseph tottered across the room on cricket-thin legs and picked up a chair that was far too bulky for his bent frame to carry. Byron hurried forward to relieve the valet.

The valet grunted as the chair left his hands and hobbled back to his seat at the foot of his master's bed. Byron placed the chair a safe distance from the bed and sat down.

His father peered at him with eyes so faded in color and void of power that Byron almost felt sorry for him, but then a ghost of the old familiar sneer appeared on the man's thinned lips, and Byron recoiled.

"A schoolmaster…teaching b-books to boys." He spat out the words, and Byron knew he'd been saving his energy for this last insult. "I gave you the best—The King's School, Cambridge—" He wheezed and paused to gulp some air as though sucking nectar from a straw. "And you…" He left the sentence unfinished, the effort of speaking requiring more energy than was stored in his decaying body.

"Why did you call me here, Father? What is it you want from me after all these years of disappointing you?"

"You abandoned me," the old man rasped. "Your duty as a son. I gave you…"

Byron stood, his body seething with rage. "If you expect an apology from me, you will get none, so if that is all you have to say, then I will take my leave. I believe Bessie has some custard pies waiting for me in the kitchen."

His father focused his filmy gray eyes on his son's face. "It's—"

he sucked in some more nectar—"all yours now."

"What are you talking about?"

"The house…my empire…all yours."

"It's not mine, nor do I want it. You disinherited me years ago, remember? I do not want your money or any part of your business."

"You must…my work…my name." A momentary flash of anger sparked his father's eyes to life. "Your duty."

"I owe you nothing," Byron spoke through gritted teeth.

"I gave you the best—public school, Cambridge…"

Byron leaned close to his father's face. "You killed my mother, you brute. My brother never got the chance to take a breath because of what you did to her. I don't want any part of you. Do you hear me?"

"You must." He latched onto Byron with his gnarled hand. "My legacy…I built it from nothing. Keep my name alive."

Byron jerked back, repulsed. His father's arm flopped down with a thud. He blinked up at Byron. Then his head rolled to the side like a dead weight. The man's eyes stared lifelessly at nothing. Anger boiled inside Byron's chest. The bastard showed no remorse, even at the end.

He turned to look at Joseph, who sagged in his chair, snoring. *What will you do now, Joseph? With your Master tyrant dead and gone?*

"Joseph," he snapped.

The old dog opened a sleepy eye.

"Your master is dead."

"Dead?" Joseph bolted upright in his seat.

"That's right, Joseph, dead. You're finally free. As am I."

Joseph blinked and made no move to check on his master. He wore a blank expression as though he had no idea what to do next, and Byron suspected that, with his master buried, the ancient valet would lay his head down and go to sleep forever.

"WHY DID YOU stay in the bastard's employ for so long, Bessie?" Byron sat, a bottle of brandy in hand, with his back pressed against the stone wall of the kitchen.

Bessie picked up the tea tray and carried it to the rough wooden table. "First, I stayed for your Mama, and then I stayed for you." She placed a tea tray next to Byron's untouched custard tart and busied herself with pouring two cups of tea. "After that, I'd been in your father's employ for too long, and he said he'd blacken my name to any future employers if I left, so I stayed." She sat next to Byron and dropped two sugar lumps into her tea.

"Bastard! Well, you're free now. I'll give you a glowing reference. You'll be able to get a job at the palace." Byron raised his brandy bottle to cheer Bessie's newfound liberty. "Get a glass and let's drink to it!"

"Why not celebrate with tea?" Bessie drew her cup to her lip as Byron swallowed another swig of brandy.

The housekeeper's brow creased. "Surely, I won't need to move on now that you'll be back, Master Byron. I have long looked forward to the day that you'd come home and fill this place with a family of your own. Make it joyful again."

"Joyful *again*?" Byron smirked. "When was this Bastille—" he gestured to the space around him—"ever joyful?"

"When your mama was alive." Bessie's eyes misted over. "You filled the house with laughter when she played with you— the times when your papa was away, traveling for business. Do you remember that?"

"You mean before he beat her to death?" A bitter gall rose in Byron's throat.

Lowering her gaze, Bessie fiddled with the handle of her teacup as though wishing to distract herself. "The doctor said she died giving birth to her stillborn babe. The child came too early, and your mother bled too much."

"You don't have to protect me any longer, Bessie. I know he made it happen."

She turned to him, her eyes full of pain. "How do you know

that?"

Byron's body went rigid, and suddenly he was five again, crouching in the corner of his bedroom.

"Ungrateful, harlot! You'll do as I say." His father, grabbing his mother by the shoulders and flinging her across the room. His mother, hitting the wall and slumping to the floor, as a stain of dark blood blossomed across her dress...

Byron squeezed his eyes shut as the horror flooded back to him. "I saw him. And I did nothing to stop him. I did nothing to help her. I stayed crouched in the corner, watching her bleed."

"Don't blame yourself for his sins." Bessie gripped his arm, forcing him to pay attention. "Listen to me. You were a mere child of five. What could you have done?"

"You're right. I was helpless then and helpless again when my wife and babe died. I failed to protect those I loved the most." He gulped more brandy and took comfort in the burn it left in his throat and chest.

"You did not fail. As far as I know, no man can outwit typhus." Bessie sat back and wrapped her hands around her teacup as if drawing comfort from the warmth. "Your father was a monster, but you cannot let him keep hurting you. He is dead, and your mama's dying wish was for your future happiness. Give her that."

Byron put his bottle of brandy down, rested his forearms on the wooden table, and gazed at the flames that darted about in the cooking range.

"The gods do not seem to be on my side, Bessie."

"What gods do you speak of, Master Byron? I am certain God wants everyone to be happy."

Byron dropped his head into his hands. Was he that different from his father? He had treated Violet appallingly, and he'd been living in a state of angry bitterness since Olivia's death. The realization brought with it a feeling of nausea. *As if life singled me out for misery. As if countless others have not suffered a thousand more pains than I have.* He'd resolved not to be like his father, yet he was in danger of turning into the same beast without even realizing it.

Bessie put her hand on his arm. "I'm only a servant, Master Byron, and I do not have the wisdom of a Cambridge-educated young man, but I am not without life experience, and I think at the root of your misery lies a young lady."

Removing his hands from his face, Byron turned to her and sighed. "You are wise indeed, Bessie."

"What's her name?"

"What does it matter?" Byron said. "I tied myself to the wrong woman for the wrong reasons, and now the woman I love despises me."

"Tied yourself? Are you married, Master Byron?"

"I'm set to be, but I have since changed my mind. The girl is with child."

Bessie gasped.

"It's not mine."

"Well, then." She exhaled. "You need not shoulder another man's responsibilities. Let this unwed mother marry the father of her child, and free yourself to pursue the one you love."

"It's too late; she detests me."

"It's never too late. I promise you that this woman, whoever she is, does not detest you."

"How could you possibly know, Bessie?"

"You forget that I am a woman too. And believe it or not, I was once young. I promise you that the problem lies not with this young lady but within yourself. You jeopardize your own happiness because deep down, you believe yourself undeserving."

Byron reached for the brandy, but Bessie moved the bottle out of his grasp. She nodded at Byron's teacup. "Drink it. You've had nothing but brandy in your stomach these last three days.

He picked up his teacup and drained it, grimacing at the taste of the now-cold liquid. He poured himself a fresh cup. Bessie was right. He had tasted happiness twice in his life—first with Olivia and then again with Violet—and he had liked the taste of it. Yet, he'd let Violet slip away.

No, he'd chased her away with his foolishness. Why had he ever consented to marry Amelia? It wasn't for the money or the position as headmaster. It was as Bessie had said—deep down, he felt he deserved punishing—for becoming frozen with fear and doing nothing to protect his mother on that fateful day and for failing to protect his beloved Olivia and their sweet babe. For years, he'd nursed the lie that these deaths were his fault, but now he saw how foolish such thinking was. It was time to let go of this incorrectly placed guilt. His father's wrongdoings were not his responsibility, and he was tired of paying the penalty.

CHAPTER TWENTY-THREE

Soul meets soul on lovers' lips.

—Percy Bysshe Shelley, "Prometheus Unbound"

"WHAT IS IT?" Violet looked up from her translation of Homer to see Ottilie smiling at her from her position on the sofa.

"Nothing." Ottilie feigned ignorance, but the smile continued to play on her lips.

"Aren't you supposed to be reading—" she glanced at the open book in Ottilie's hands—"Darwin, is it?"

Ottilie closed her book. "I feel a little restless today, that's all." She stood and walked to the mullioned window that looked out onto Aunt Prudence's town garden.

"I'm restless too." Violet put away her ink pen and joined her friend. "I know, I shouldn't, but I keep thinking about Mr. Thomas. I cannot believe how badly Miss Farthington used him—eloping to France with a baron while he was away tending to his dying father. And what of her flirtation with that odious Monsieur L'Strang?"

"I am not at all surprised."

"About Miss Farthington eloping to France? Or about her leaving the lecherous Monsieur L'Strang to his wife?"

"Either one. I think Miss Farthington is the type of woman

who keeps many secret lovers. And now that she has secured herself a French baron, she can play at being a lady of propriety."

"Do you think she can become one?"

Ottilie shook her head. "Definitely not. She will play the part for a while, and then she will return to her old tricks. But at least she managed to save her mother's reputation. There will be talk, but it will die out quickly. Marrying a baron—even a French one—isn't disastrous enough to warrant a large scandal."

"Yes, and she will have her baby in France, so no one will be the wiser about when she conceived." Violet picked at the sleeve of her dress, pausing in thought before broaching what truly bothered her. "What part do you think Mr. Thomas played in her schemes? Do you think she ever loved him?"

"Of course not. Amelia used him as a cover for her wayward deeds abroad. She needed him in the event none of her lovers relented and married her."

"So, you believe he is not the father of her child?" Hope swelled in Violet's chest. She wanted, more than anything, for that to be true.

"I am certain he is not." The conviction in Ottilie's tone surprised Violet. Her friend had been so infuriated with Byron these past weeks that she'd hardly dared mention his name. What had changed?

She looked out onto the garden. The day was bright with summer cheer, but it was not enough to cheer her thoughts, which lingered on a dark evening in a very different garden.

"How can you be so certain? How can anyone be?"

"Trust me." Ottilie put a gentle hand on Violet's arm.

"That night, at the party, he stopped me in the garden and told me that he did not love Miss Farthington. He insisted he'd been coerced into agreeing to the marriage and swore the child wasn't his. But when I asked him how he could be sure, he could not answer." Violet pressed her lips together. Tears pricked her eyes.

"Is that what plagues you?" Ottilie asked.

"It doesn't plague me." Violet turned her face to the ceiling.

"Violet, I hear you cry into your pillow at night. I know."

A tear rolled down Violet's cheek. "I just wish the pain would subside, but it is relentless." She turned back to Ottilie, "What am I going to do?"

"You must talk to him."

"How? He has been gone near two months, and it does not appear that he will ever return."

"He will, and when he does, I am certain he will come to you." Ottilie's eyes twinkled, and her cheeks dimpled as a smile formed on her lips.

"You're doing it again." Anxiety made Violet snap the words.

"What?"

"Acting as though you're hiding a secret. Do you have something to tell me?"

"Only this—" Ottilie reached for Violet's hands—"Remember that I am your true friend and that my greatest wish is for your happiness. If I have ever misjudged your intentions or questioned your decisions in the past, I am sorry."

"Do not apologize," Violet said, shaking her head. "You have been nothing short of the truest friend without whom I would surely have been lost."

Ottilie threw her arms around Violet's neck. "Dearest Violet, promise me you will open your mind and choose happiness."

"I will, and you must promise me the same." Violet closed her arms around her friend.

EVERY NERVE IN Byron's body sang. He stood rigid in the hallway as he waited for Lady Astyr's butler to return, but inside, his emotions ran wild. It had been almost two months since he'd laid eyes on Violet, and she'd been furious with him during their last meeting. He did not expect her to forgive him, but he to let her know how he felt. He had to speak, or he'd regret it for the rest of his life.

After several agonizing minutes, the butler returned.

"Miss Greyson will receive you in the study." He emphasized the word *study* as if to express his disapproval of this informal meeting place.

"Thank you." Byron followed the man up a grand staircase. He'd been surprised to learn that Violet had an aunt in Mayfair, but he was utterly floored by the grandeur of her home. Why had she kept this information hidden and presented herself as a penniless orphan? Perhaps, she'd done so for the same reasons he'd kept his father and his family's wealth a secret.

The butler stopped outside the study and pushed open the door. Byron's stomach tightened as the servant announced his presence, "Mr. Byron Thomas."

As he stepped into the room, Violet looked up from where she sat at her writing desk, and their eyes met. His pulse raced. He hadn't realized how much he'd missed her—how much he'd longed to see her face again and hold her in his arms. She put down her quill and wiped her hands before standing up to greet him.

"Violet." He strode forward, wanting to close the distance between them, but she dropped her gaze and smoothed the sides of her blue dress as though uncertain what to do with her hands.

He paused to gather his emotions. Then, clearing his throat, he said, "May I still call you Violet?"

She wrapped her arms around herself in a protective gesture and avoided answering his question. "I was sorry to hear about the cancellation of your engagement."

Byron frowned. He hated the formality with which she spoke to him. "Were you?"

"Of course. Miss Farthington behaved abominably toward you—no one deserves that kind of treatment."

Byron stepped closer, determined to break the wall of formality she'd erected. "And you think that upset me? Because I loved her and wanted to marry her?"

"I—I do not know. Did you?"

Byron could see that tears pooled in Violet's eyes. He moved to comfort her but stopped when he saw her body flinch. Fear flooded his veins. *Did she truly believe that he was sorry to have lost Amelia Farthington?* He rubbed his jaw. He had to make her understand, or she would be lost to him.

"Violet, I meant what I said in the garden that night, I never loved Amelia, and I did not want to marry her. I am thrilled that she found herself a baron and left that monster L'Strang behind. In doing so, she helped to salvage her mother's reputation, and that is the only reason I agreed to marry Amelia. Even radicals must draw the line somewhere."

She clasped her hands together. "So why are you here? Is it on behalf of Headmistress Briggs? Do you want me to return to Westminster Ladies' College after summer?"

"I have resigned my position at St. James's, and I will be leaving Westminster College, too."

"Oh." She hadn't anticipated this, and it shocked her. "Where will you go?"

"That depends on you," he said.

"Me?"

He stepped forward and clasped her gently by the shoulders so that he could look her in the eye. "You do not understand. I love you. I came here today to ask for your hand in marriage."

"I—I cannot. It is too soon."

He released his hold on her and stepped back. "What do you mean 'too soon'?"

Her chin trembled. "I mean, there are still too many unanswered questions."

"Regarding Amelia?"

Violet fixed her blue eyes on him and nodded.

"I have already told you that I did not love her. Mr. and Mrs. Briggs coerced me into proposing to her because she was with child and the college's reputation was in jeopardy."

Violet's body flinched at the mention of Amelia's pregnancy as though it stung her. *So that is the cause of her resistance, he thought.* "Amelia's child is not mine," he said firmly. "I courted her and flirted with the idea of marrying her before I met you, not because I cared for her, but because Mr. Briggs said the marriage would secure my place as headmaster of St. James's after his retirement. She took advantage of that fact and told her parents the child was mine. I knew it wasn't, but I felt obligated and cornered. The scandal would have ruined Headmistress Briggs and her school." He paused. "It would have ruined your future too."

"So, you were going to marry Amelia to save my future?" Anger crept into Violet's voice.

He shrugged. "In part. It's foolish, I know it sounds feeble, but after my wife and child perished, I no longer believed in love. I'd become a bitter man, like my father. But I would never have gone through with the wedding–not after I saw you in the garden that night. I came to realize that I was sabotaging my happiness. That's something I've been doing for years. But I do not want to do it any longer."

"And did you lie with Amelia for my sake, too?"

Byron paled. Violet's accusation caught him off guard. "Who told you that?'

"You did, that night in the garden."

"I told you that I'd lain with Amelia?"

Violet hesitated. "You did not deny it."

"I see." Byron nodded and took a deep breath to steady his nerves. "Something did happen, but I can assure you that it is not what you think."

She folded her arms and turned away from him.

He spoke quickly then, determined not to lose her again. "I'd been drinking brandy—a lot of it—and I kept slipping in and out of consciousness. At some point, Amelia came into the library, and when I woke up, she was—on top of me. I managed to push her off. At first, my memory was unclear, but the incident has since become clearer in my mind. I recall that she was furious and accused me of not being man enough."

Violet sank onto the chair next to her writing desk and buried her face in her hands.

A dark cloud of despair settled over Byron. "I know my transgressions hurt you, and I cannot fault you if you are unable to find it in your heart to forgive me. But I want you to know that I am sorry for ever causing you a moment's pain and that I wish for nothing more than your happiness." He continued looking at Violet, hoping she'd lift her eyes and react to his words, but her head remained bowed. He sighed. "I see now that I cannot make you happy, and that is reason enough for me to leave you be."

Byron turned, his heart sitting heavy in his chest, and moved toward the door.

Then he felt her light touch on his arm. He spun around.

"I do forgive you," she said. "How could I not when losing you makes the world look three shades darker?

"Thank God." Byron pulled her toward him and buried his face in her neck, inhaling her sweet rose scent. "I thought I'd lost you forever."

"I did too." Violet turned her face and sought out his mouth with her lips.

Byron gripped her waist and kissed her deeply. When they parted, he caressed her face and traced his thumb across her mouth, "'soul meets soul on lovers' lips'," he whispered, "now I truly understand what Shelley meant."

"Yes," Violet smiled and rested her head against his chest.

EPILOGUE

August 1862
Canterbury, England

"THE OLD SCROOGE would turn over in his grave if he knew that I sold his business and used the proceeds to further the education of women," Byron said and squeezed his wife's hand.

Violet looked up at her husband and smiled. "But your mother would be so proud, as would mine."

They stood together and watched the stonemason finish etching the final "e" on the new sign that sat above the entrance to the stone building that was Byron's former home: *Canterbury Ladies' College.*

As soon as the mason started making his way down the ladder, applause broke out.

"It looks wonderful," Ottilie said.

"I am glad you think so, Miss Hamilton. As head of the mathematics and science departments, your opinion is vital." Byron smiled.

Ottilie grinned. "Oh, I am so pleased with the new science laboratory."

"You can thank Aunt Prudence for that." Violet reached for her aunt's hand. "She is an important patron of this academy and women's education."

"That is right." Aunt Prudence's face lit up. "Violet has transformed my thinking, and I am now quite the radical."

"Hear, hear," Mrs. Briggs said. "May ladies' colleges spring up all over the country."

"You two have done a fine job turning this old building around." Mr. Briggs gazed at the building and nodded his approval. "And when your establishment opens, I hope you will count on this retired principal as being a frequent visiting lecturer."

"We will certainly hold you to that promise, Mr. Briggs. Your expertise will be most welcome," Violet said.

"How many students are you expecting in September?" Mrs. Briggs asked.

"Fifteen-day students and ten borders."

"Five-and-twenty young ladies to care for." Bessie rubbed her hands together. "I shall enjoy that."

"And one little lady or lad." Violet placed her hand on her growing bump and glanced at her husband.

Byron met her gaze, put his arm around her shoulders, and let out a deep and contented sigh.

Author's Note

Love and Literature is a homage to Charlotte Bronte's first novel, *The Professor,* published posthumously in 1857, and its reworking *Villette,* published in 1853. Likely the least-read of Charlotte's novels, *The Professor* has always been amongst my favorites because I believe it's close to Charlotte's heart and strongly influenced much of her later work.

From 1842-1844, Charlotte was a student and teacher at the *Pensionnat Héger* in Brussels. During her time at the school, she developed a close bond, and subsequently an infatuation, with her professor, Constantin Héger, husband to the headmistress and father of six children. After returning to England in 1844, while suffering the pain of unrequited love, Charlotte wrote several passionate letters to Monsieur Héger and started working on *The Professor,* which she completed in 1846. In a letter dated November 1845, Charlotte describes her torment to Héger, writing, "I am in a fever—I lose my appetite and my sleep—I pine away."

Anyone interested in learning more about this fascinating period in Charlotte's life should read her surviving letters to Monsieur Héger, available on the British Library Website.

Inspired by Charlotte's novel, *Love and Literature* explores the adult-student/professor romance trope in conjunction with the emergence of higher education for women in Victorian England. As such, *Love and Literature* also pays homage to the forward-thinking feminists who pioneered higher education for women by founding and funding the first academic ladies' colleges in England. Some of the women who inspired this series include Elizabeth Jesser Reid, who opened Bedford College in 1849 for the education of non-conformist women; Dorothea Beale, who was headmistress of Cheltenham Ladies' College; Frances Mary Buss, who founded North London Collegiate School in 1850 for middle-class girls; and Emily Davies, who founded Girton College in 1869, and who, together with Frances Buss, successfully persuaded Cambridge to allow women to sit for their Local Examinations.[1]

Many of these women were graduates of Queen's College, founded in 1843 to elevate the education of governesses. But the struggle for women's education did not end with the emergence of the first ladies' colleges. Teaching academics to women for the sake of learning was controversial. These pioneers of higher education for women faced immense hurdles, used their personal funds, and repeatedly had to prove their worth.

I chose to set *Love and Literature* in 1861, a time when the interest in women's education was growing, but well after the first ladies' colleges had opened. I did this to separate my fictional college from association with any historical colleges (many of which still exist today) and my characters from historical figures. All my characters are fictional, and none of my creations represent any real person or institution.

---

[1] Ridley, A. (1895). *Frances Mary Buss and Her Work for Education*. Longmans, Green, & Co.

ABOUT THE AUTHOR

Aviva holds a master's degree in English and has a keen interest in British literature. She is an anglophile and Brontë enthusiast who is happiest when traveling to or writing about England. Inspiration for her first book, The Mist on Brontë Moor, came after she visited the Brontë Parsonage in Haworth.

Born and raised in Cape Town, South Africa, Aviva now lives in Southern California with her husband, two daughters, and rambunctious Yorkshire terrier—named for the oft-forgotten Brontë brother Branwell.

Website: www.avivaorrauthor.com
Twitter: twitter.com/aviva_orr
Facebook: facebook.com/AuthorAvivaOrr
Goodreads: goodreads.com/author/show/6464067.Aviva_Orr
Bookbub: bookbub.com/profile/aviva-orr

* 9 7 8 1 9 6 0 1 8 4 6 0 3 *